Beyond
Mist Blue
Mountains

Books by Carrie Bender

Miriam's Journal
A Fruitful Vine
A Winding Path
A Joyous Heart
A Treasured Friendship
A Golden Sunbeam

Dora's Diary
Birch Hollow Schoolmarm
Lilac Blossom Time
Beyond Mist Blue Mountains

Whispering Brook Series
Whispering Brook Farm
Summerville Days
Chestnut Ridge Acres
Hemlock Hill Hideaway
Woodland Dell's Secret
Timberlane Cove

Dora's Diary
3

Beyond Mist Blue Mountains

Carrie Bender

Herald Press

Scottdale, Pennsylvania
Waterloo, Ontario

Library of Congress Cataloging-in-Publication Data
Bender, Carrie, 1953-
  Beyond mist blue mountains / Carrie Bender.
    p. cm. — (Dora's diary ; 3)
  ISBN 0-8361-9165-X (alk. paper)
  1. Women missionaries—Fiction. 2. Adopted children—Fiction.
3. Married women—Fiction. 4. Childlessness—Fiction.
5. Belize—Fiction. I. Title.
  PS3552.E53845B495 2003
  813'.54—dc21

2003001812

This story is fiction, but true to Amish life. Any resemblance to persons living or dead is coincidental.

Scripture is adapted from *The King James Version*.

BEYOND MIST BLUE MOUNTAINS
Copyright © 2003 by Herald Press, Scottdale, Pa. 15683
    Published simultaneously in Canada by Herald Press,
    Waterloo, Ont. N2L 6H7. All rights reserved
Library of Congress Catalog Number: 2003001812
International Standard Book Number: 0-8361-9165-X
Printed in the United States of America
Art by Joy Dunn Keenan
Book design by Paula Johnson and Sandra Johnson

11 10 09 08 07 06 05 04 03 10 9 8 7 6 5 4 3 2 1

To order or request information, please call
1-800-759-4447 (individuals); 1-800-245-7894 (trade).
Website: www.mph.org

Contents

Millstream Orchard Farm

....

This finds me sitting on the porch at the Millstream Orchard Farm, enjoying the beauties of the spring-like evening. We're having a few days of unseasonably warm weather. A pair of robins found their way here and are cheerfully chirping from the old apple trees in the orchard. We spent this beautiful afternoon trimming the gnarled old overgrown and tangled twigs and branches from the neglected apple trees, and raked them into piles. Matthew's out there now with the horses and wagons loading up the twigs to take them out to the field to be burned. We don't expect much of a crop of apples, as the trees are too old and too long neglected, but there should be enough for us and all the neighbors, too.

We've been very busy these past few days, for our plans changed drastically, all in a short time. We had been building up our hopes and dreams of going to Belize to help Matthew's uncle and aunt, Cephas and Barbara Bontrager, in their orphanage, being substitute parents to motherless and fatherless children. We were eagerly awaiting their letter and starting to make plans to go. When the letter arrived it was a let-down, for they wrote that the couple managing the orphanage now have decided to stay awhile longer—at least until fall—but they want us to come then, as soon as they leave. That meant we'd have to find ourselves a place to live—and a job for Matthew. A few days later the new owner of this farm stopped in, wondering if anyone would be interested in renting it for a year, until he is ready to take over. His own plans had changed, too, and he had to postpone his plans of farming it this spring. Of course, we were delighted to have the chance, and so we'll be spending the first summer of our married life on a farm after all. It made us awfully busy— Matthew and his dad and brothers have been making repairs in the barn and fixing things up. Since it will be only for one growing season, we won't fix up the dairy and milk cows, and neighbor Enos Miller has offered to let Matthew use his farm implements, so only a few basic items have to be bought.

Matthew's sisters, Rosabeth and Anna Ruth, helped me to clean and scrub the whole house, from the cupola on top down to the cobwebby cellar. We're really thankful now, after all, for all the papering and painting we did when we thought this farm would be ours. The owner consented to pay for new linoleum in the kitchen if we install it. Matthew did a good job of it, and I can hardly believe it's the same little kitchen I first saw when Miss Sophie lived here. Then things looked incredibly old and worn, but now, with the kitchen cabinets painted white, the shiny, new checkered linoleum, the woodwork redone, the walls covered with fresh new wallpaper, and the old cook stove polished and shined until it fairly gleams, it almost looks like my kitchen of dreams!

I can hardly believe that we have a home of our own at last! Be it ever so humble, there is no place like home! Time to quit writing, for we have a busy day planned for tomorrow, and Matthew's coming in with the horses now.

March 8
....
Our unseasonable spring-like weather continues, and Matthew has already begun to plow the fields, knowing full well that by a week from today all could be under a blanket of snow again. I went outside to inspect the buds on the lilac bushes in the front yard after dinner, and just then the mail carrier came chugging up the hill and stopped at our new mailbox for the first time! It was a letter from "home"—the very first we received at our new home. Good news from a far country is as cold water to a thirsty soul. Mamm, Daed, and Sadie had written letters, and good news it was! They're coming out in a week with a driver in a rental truck and bringing all our wedding gifts and the new furniture. Then we can begin "housekeeping" for real instead of having only the kitchen and bedroom furnished.

Wouldn't it be nice if we could own this farm and

think of staying here twenty years or more? If only Miss Sophie had lived awhile longer. . . .

Matthew and I took a walk through the orchards tonight, just as the sun was setting in a maze of red and pink glory over the old apple trees and reflecting in the big pond until it glowed with color and brightness. It was one of the loveliest sunsets we'd ever seen, and our pair of robins were still around, although they haven't done more than chirp yet. I keep thinking of how lovely it will be when all the orchard is in blossom, with the sweet, fragrant, pink and white petals floating down on the breeze, and the air ringing with the melody of birdsong. The only things that might surpass the beauty of that would be when the big lilac bushes are in blossom, or the honeysuckle vines on the old wall out front. Springtime is the loveliest time of year, if we only take the time to appreciate it.

Golden Gem for Today:
Give us this day our daily bread.
O Savior, who art the Bread of Life,
evermore nourish and
strengthen our fainting souls
by imparting to them Thyself.

March 18

Our kitchen looks real homey now with our wedding gifts here: the homemade rugs, crocheted potholders, homespun tablecloth, the blue ceramic canister set, and the wooden breadbox. The stagecoach and horses set stands regally on the shelf, and I think of Clark and Mrs. Worthington when I see it. In the other rooms there are our new bedroom suites with the quilts I made on the beds, and in the *Sitzschtubb* (sitting room) is the beautiful handmade corner cupboard, the library table, and settee. It's going to *schpeid* me (make me sorry) to put it all into storage again when we leave for Belize, but I'm glad we can use it until fall, or longer.

Mamm, Daed, and Sadie have been here for three days, and left this morning. We appreciated their help on the farm, and in getting our things into place. Sadie helped me to do some more cleaning up in the yard and around the buildings, and now everything looks rather shipshape. It was a wonderful three days having them here, but all too soon it was time for them to leave and Matthew had to cheer me up. *So gates* (so it goes).

April 15

Time sure seems to fly when one is busy and happy. The beauties of springtime are delightful, and tonight Matthew and I took the time to explore our back meadow and woods. I had never been back there before and would like to go back again in a month or so, when everything will be green and the leaves will be out on the trees. There's a creek back there, too, and at one place it was real shallow, with big stepping stones across it. We crossed over, and a worn little path led around the sloping meadow. On the other side of the hill, nestled in among the trees, was a picturesque little cottage with a cobblestone walk leading to it and a white picket fence around it. There were two spruce trees, one on either side of the walk, and there was a little gate hung between the two trees, with the hinges and clasp right in the trees. The cobblestone walk led up to an inviting front door, and Matthew and I decided we would be neighborly and call on our nearest neighbors. We knocked on the door, but no one was home, so we took the liberty to follow the cobblestones around the side of the house. There was a stone bench under the trees, and two stone deer on either side, flanked by arborvitae bushes. Everything was neat as a pin and there were a lot of mulched flowerbeds encircled with rocks. It sure *schpeided* me (made me sorry) that the people weren't home, for I felt sure that interesting people must live there. But we'll try it again sometime.

May 10

The lilacs are blooming and I have a big bouquet of them in a vase on the table, perfuming the whole kitchen with their sweet fragrance. Here we had been expecting to be in far-away Belize when the lilacs bloomed, and now we're here to enjoy them after all. Matthew is busy planting corn these days and hopes to finish before it rains. We got a cute little cocker spaniel puppy from Owen Hershbergers' last week, and he is quite playful. This afternoon, Betty (Mrs. Enos Miller) had a dentist appointment in town, and dropped off Atlee and the three little girls here. They sure had fun playing with that puppy! They put a doll's cap on him, wrapped him in a doll blanket, and even put him in the doll coach and pushed him around. It was good to have some childish laughter and voices around here for a change. I finished my lawn mowing and trimming tonight, and Matthew is nearly finished in the field. I hope we find the time soon to take a walk back into our meadowland again. It is lush with green grasses, buttercups, forget-me-nots, and clover blossoms, and I'm more than a little anxious and curious to visit the people in that dear, picturesque little house nestled in the trees. I hope it's someone we can be good friends with.

May 20
.... The apple orchards are a drift of white and pink blossoms in all their glory these days, and so we find an excuse to go out there nearly every evening. If Matthew doesn't have the time, I go alone. It won't last long—we must enjoy it while we can. It's a haven for birds; the melodious chorus is almost heavenly out there. Tonight while I was sitting in the orchard working on a friendship patch for a quilt that the community is making for a family that is moving out of state this

fall, I happened to spy a movement down in the meadow. Someone was coming across the stepping stones in the creek and making her way through the meadow grasses and wildflowers—a woman wearing a big floppy sun hat and a dress with a long, flowing skirt. When she spied me sitting there in the orchard, she waved and headed my way. When she came closer I noticed that she had silvery white hair encircling a round, pink-cheeked face, and friendly, merry brown eyes—a kindly soul by the looks of her. She promptly made herself at home, sitting down on the orchard grass, admiring the patch I was making, and chattering away as if we'd have been old friends for years. She introduced herself as Mrs. Jocelyn Bates. She lives with her husband, Ken, in that quaint little cottage over yonder meadow! She's a friendly, interesting person, the kind that everyone likes right away, and I hope we'll be good friends as long as we're neighbors. She invited us to try to pay them a visit again soon, and they're going to come visit us, together, sometime, too.

May 25
....

It feels like summer has arrived, for it's barefoot weather, over eighty degrees. Things are growing by leaps and bounds. Matthew has consented to our going to visit Jocelyn and Ken tonight, and I'm looking forward to both the lovely walk and the visit. This afternoon we explored the musty old mill. It's an interesting place, or rather,

I'm sure that at one time it was. I'm not altogether sure how it worked, but I think there's a big water-wheel underneath the mill that water in the millrace powered, and it turned the big dog wheels that spun the millstones, which ground the grain into flour. I suppose that one day this mill was a busy, prosperous place with men coming with wagon loads of grain pulled by big, heavy workhorses. The deep millrace is no longer very full, and low bushes grow along its banks on both sides. It's an excellent place for birds and wildlife—I saw muskrats dive into the water, frogs jumping to safety, and bunnies and woodchucks scrambling for cover. When our little cocker pup gets a little bigger, he'll probably have a heyday going after them.

It's time to get supper on the table—we're having our first meal of strawberries and I made a shortcake to go with them.

Golden Gem for Today:
Love is one of the fruits of the Spirit, and fruits
are produced and ripened by slow degrees.
We cannot command our feelings
as we can our actions, but we can,
with the help of God, and through much prayer
to Him and by careful cultivation,
cast out unloving feelings and replace them
with Christ-like love.

Last night after the evening chores were done we set out through the backfield lane to the lovely buttercup-filled meadowland. Most everything was green, green, green, except the sky and treetops and trunks, or so it seemed. It's beautiful back there, and I would've loved to spend the evening exploring. We crossed the creek on the stepping stones and soon came in sight of the Bates' lovely little cottage. This time they were home, sitting on the quaint stone bench with the deer on either side, and they welcomed us as old friends. Ken is a handsome man with snow-white hair, although his face is unlined, and with a likeable personality. He brought out wooden rockers for us to sit on beside their delightful little garden and interesting flowerbeds, a mixture of perennials and annuals. We had a lovely visit, and then Jocelyn told us some of their life story and why they moved to this out-of-the-way place. She said that thirty years ago they had a little boy—her voice broke as she talked of how dear and sweet he was, with big, trusting blue eyes and a head full of blond curls. He was the joy of their life—and then one day when he was twenty months old, Jocelyn left an open bottle of her prescription medicine on the counter and forgot all about it. She went into another room, and when she came back the little boy had climbed up and swallowed the pills, which he probably mistook for candy. They rushed him to the hospital, unconscious, where they worked on him and were able to pull him through. But his brain had been too long without oxygen and there was severe damage. He was like a newborn infant after that, completely helpless. Jocelyn went through a hard time of not being able to forgive herself and of not wanting anyone to know about it, so they moved to the little cottage, far away from any of their acquaintances. Their son lived for ten more years, during which time she devoted herself entirely to caring for the invalid, taking no time for a social life and allowing none of the few friends she made here to see or know about her son. After his death, she began to realize how wrong her attitude had been and how she had been closing her heart to friendship and to God's love and forgiveness. She said she's trying to make up for lost time now; she's doing all she can to help others and is involved in a lot of volunteer work.

They told us about their next-door neighbor, a half mile closer to the main road north of them. He is an interesting old man, who for some unknown reason goes by the name of Colonel Dick, probably a nickname from his younger days. They offered to take us to visit him sometime. They said he's a very friendly old man whom they are sure we'd enjoy meeting, and of course, we accepted their offer.

It was a delightful evening, and walking home in the darkness with only flashlights to light our paths (for there was no moon) was rather thrilling. A few times our flashlight beams reflected the gleaming eyes of some animal as it slunk away in the bushes, and we heard rustlings and the pattering of little feet in the thickets. It gave me a shivery feeling, but I felt safe with Matthew there to keep the wild creatures at bay.

June 22

Happiness is:
Having a bouquet of beautiful heavenly-scented
    red roses on the kitchen table
Getting a fat pack of letters from "home"
Getting the berries picked, the garden hoed,
    and the hay all baled before it rains
Finding the lost scissors behind the cushion
    on the Boston rocker
Getting an invitation to Matthew's parents' place
    for supper on Sunday evening
Hearing a bluebird sweetly singing
Baking an angel food cake and having it
    turn out high, light, and fluffy
Having the counter full of jars of strawberry jam,
    and finding that every one of them has sealed
Having Betty Miller and the children stop in
    for a friendly chat
Seeing Matthew coming in the walk with
    a bouquet of June lilies

July 28

Matthew is glad that the threshing is over and that the farm work has temporarily slowed down a bit. He brought in a hat full of wild black raspberries he had picked in the fencerow, and I went out with a dishpan and searched the thickets and hedgerows until I found enough to make several batches of jelly. It was worth getting my arms scratched a bit, for I could do some bird watching at the same time and found quite a few nests.

Last evening we took the time to visit Jocelyn and Ken again—this time we went the long way round with Captain hitched to the *Dachweggeli* (roofed buggy). They were both interested in having a carriage ride so we took them for a drive, and I saw some of the countryside I'd never seen before. Jocelyn and I sat on the back seat, and I think she enjoyed it, although she got a bit nervous when Captain shied from a noisy motorcycle. On the way back we stopped in to visit Colonel Dick and found him to have a kindly heart. He was once six feet tall, but he's somewhat stooped now and his face weather-beaten. But his eyes are still twinkly. He knows a lot of history about these parts. We were very interested to learn that his grandfather was at one time the caretaker of the old mill at our place, and that he himself spent many a day on that farm when he was barely old enough to remember. He promised to come and visit us sometime, for he's interested in taking a tour of the old mill. His wife died ten years ago and their children all live in other states, so he has many a lonely evening. His house is old and in need of repairs, and maybe on a rainy day we can go over and Matthew can fix things up a bit for him. I can do some cooking and cleaning for him. We found him so interesting that we forgot the time and it was real late when we got home. Turning in the lane, by the battery lights of the carriage, we saw a mother opossum scampering away with a whole bunch of little ones clinging to her tail. The moon was shining, and over by the orchard we saw a doe and a fawn bounding away into the spruce woods. I suppose they're waiting for the apples in the orchard to ripen. The windfall will be a feast to them.

August 27
....
Signs of the approaching autumn can be seen here and there. Oh, where has the summer flown? Silo filling time is approaching, but we won't have to worry about that, as Matthew has sold all his crops in the field. We had a letter from Uncle Cephas and Aunt Barbara Bontrager. They wrote that their helpers in the orphanage are staying until late winter or early spring, and so we'll have some more time here in our cozy home on the dear orchard farm.

We're getting excited, though, about our planned adventure, and are thinking of making a trip back east to *Mamm* and *Daed* (Mom and Dad) first, for it seems so long since we've seen them all. Then we'll hunt up Mrs. Worthington and Clark and see about that wedding gift she promised us. We know she won't be satisfied without giving us a lot, and we might as well make good use of it—toward our fare in traveling to Belize. I picked three bushels of lima beans this morning and Matthew's going to help me hull them. His sisters, Rosabeth and Anna Ruth, are coming over, too. That will be fun!

Golden Gem for Today:
Though thou fallest often—yea
many times a day, yet as many times rise again,
and thou wilt find Me nigh.
Thou shalt know that He which hath begun
a good work in thee will perform it unto the end.
Though thou fallest, yet shalt thou not
be cast away, for I will uphold thee
with Mine Hand.

September 21

Apple picking time has begun, and there is a better yield than we had expected. I think the old-fashioned kinds are the best, and the orchard is a pleasant place to be these days. We were both up on ladders picking apples and enjoying the blue of the September skies and the apple scented breezes, when we spied a stoop-shouldered figure using a cane come walking up the path from the meadow. It was Colonel Dick, come to see the old mill and to pay us a visit! We took him all through the mill and he took a keen interest in it all—he even said he'd enjoy having his living quarters in what used to be the old office. There's a picture window there that looks out over the orchards, ponds, and spruce woods, and while we were standing there looking at the scenery, a big stately buck with a magnificent rack walked into the orchard, nibbling on apples under the trees. Colonel Dick remembered some of the things in the mill and around the farm from when he spent his summers here with his grandpa before he went to school. We invited him to stay for supper, and he accepted graciously, saying that his own cooking is far from gourmet, and that just snacking on packaged foods gets to be tiresome after awhile. Right after supper he went on his stoop-shouldered way, carrying a bag of Russet apples and thanking us for our hospitality.

October 14
....

Matthew's been taking spring-wagon loads of apples to the press to be juiced into cider. They're not nice enough to sell and wouldn't keep over the winter, but make delicious, tangy cider. I've been canning all that we can't use or give away right away, so that next winter we can have cider with doughnuts when the snows and winds are howling outside. Every now and then Matthew takes time off to go out with his gun and brings home a few pheasants, which I prepare in the roasting pan stuffed with bread filling. Or sometimes several squirrels, which I bake in barbecue sauce. One morning he woke me early, told me to get dressed and come with him—he wanted to show me something. The morning air was crisp and chilly, and a rosy glow in the east betokened the rising of the sun. We walked back into the meadowland through the frost-stiffened grasses, and followed the creek to where there was a wide pool with a beaver dam in it. At Matthew's bidding, we hid behind an evergreen thicket, keeping our eyes on the pool. It seemed like a long, chilly wait, but when the sun's rays began to glimmer on the water I suddenly noticed a piece of wood seemingly moving across the pool by itself. Then a brown, furry head emerged behind it, with ripples on the water all around it. A beaver! It surfaced, and we saw the powerful strokes of its hind legs as it guided the wood. It was then that a movement on the bank caught our attention—an otter with long whiskers was rising up on its hind legs. Breathlessly, we watched as it sniffed the chilly air and looked intently at the movement in the water. Then, quick as a flash, it soundlessly dove in—its long body sliding noiselessly over the surface before it disappeared with scarcely a ripple. The beaver in the pool threw its tail into the air and brought it down with a resounding smack, then disappeared from sight. Apparently the otter's attack wasn't successful, for there was no sign of a scuffle, and after awhile the ripples in the pool were gone and all was quiet. Watching that was well worth the chilly wait— it was even better than Matthew had expected to show me, for he hadn't known there were otters around. On the way back we saw the same magnificent buck bound away into the thickets. He's been living on our apples for awhile now and very likely is corn-fed, too. Matthew's aiming to take him as his trophy buck when the season opens. We're in need of meat, and the deer population is plentiful.

Our first anniversary. Matthew has set up a small woodworking shop out in the mill and he's been working on some mysterious project while I worked at my fall housecleaning. This morning, with the Miller boys' help, he brought it into the house—a beautifully handcrafted and varnished dry sink! Maybe someday I'll be able to use it as a baby's changing table, but for now I'll have to be satisfied with using it to display houseplants. Matthew thought we could set it in the *Sitzschtubb* (sitting room), but I told him I want it in the kitchen where I can enjoy it more. In a few months we go to South America and will have to put it into storage. I made three new shirts for Matthew, and he declared they were the most comfortable and well fitting ever. I suppose once we're in Belize I won't have time to sew for ourselves anymore, with a whole family of orphans to clothe.

Golden Gem for Today:
*Our divine Master, for the joy set before Him,
endured the cross, despising the shame,
experiencing the awful depths of the feeling
of being forsaken of the Father.*

After several weeks of the flurry of cookie baking, candy making, and gift wrapping, all seems rather quiet and peaceful around here. I was afraid we'd have a green (or brown) Christmas, but on the day before big fluffy flakes of white snow came swirling down, rather slowly at first, but soon they became smaller and came down faster and faster. By evening the snow was so deep I was afraid our guests wouldn't be able to come. But on Christmas morning the sun shone on the lovely snow-covered fields, trees, and woods, and the roads were excellent for sleighing. We had invited Enos Millers and Owen Hershbergers, and of course, Matthew's entire family. They all came, rosy-cheeked from their cold rides. I didn't have a turkey to roast, but Matthew had shot two wild geese in season, which we kept in the freezer locker until now. Everyone said they were every bit as good as turkey would have been. It did taste good after a steady diet of deer meat these past few weeks (although not the trophy buck).

It was an enjoyable day, but of course, my thoughts traveled back to the loved ones at "home" and to the gathering they'd be having and that we weren't able to be there. But the sadness was quickly gone when I realized that in less than two months we'll be with them for a whole week or more before we start on our long journey.

Matthew's dad read the Christmas story and we all chimed in singing a few Christmas carols. All too soon it was time for them to bundle up for their cold rides home. Tonight after supper Matthew got out our one-horse sleigh and hitched Captain to it. We covered up with carriage robes and went for a ride through the tingling cold air under the starry skies. We talked about how we wouldn't be able to enjoy such a ride once we're in the tropical climate of Belize! All in all, it was a joyous Christmas with lots to be thankful for and many blessings to count.

January 16
....
We're making plans and getting ready for our trip to Pennsylvania next month. I'm getting more excited about it every day. We've gotten permission from this farm's owner to store our furnishings and household goods in the office of the old mill (where it will be high and dry and safe) until we get back. Last evening we took time off to visit our neighbors over across the meadowlands, Jocelyn and Ken, and Colonel Dick. They've all three been over several times, and we felt it was high time to repay their visits before we leave. The first time I saw that quaint little cottage nestled among the trees I hoped that someone lived there with whom we could be good friends. We are good friends, but somehow we don't get over to see them as often as I thought we would—I suppose our interests are too different. So we donned snowshoes, bundled up against the cold, and made our way through the meadow, enjoying the wintry wonderland all around us. The creek was

frozen solid around the stepping stones, so there was no danger of slipping into the water. There were animal tracks all along the banks, so the wildlife is still abundant, even when everything's frozen. I suppose some of them are hibernating, warm and cozy in their dens, waiting for the warm spring breezes to awaken them. The lights in the windows of the little cottage welcomed us with their warm glow, and before we had a chance to knock the door was thrown open and we were given a grand welcome. Colonel Dick was there, too, and we had a happy evening of visiting and getting better acquainted. It almost *schpeids* me (makes me sorry) now to be leaving them, but maybe when we get back we can find a farm to rent somewhere in this area and continue our friendship.

On the way home the full moon was up, lighting up the snow-covered scenery almost like daylight. I told Matthew that I feel a little bit sad to be leaving this farm that has grown dear to us and that we once thought would be ours—the glorious old orchard in the spring, the spruce woods with its interesting wildlife, the meadow and creek, the old mill and millstream, the lilac bush and the old honeysuckle covered wall, and even the dear, funny cupola on top of the house. It's home to us now. But Matthew reminded me that as the saying goes, "when one door shuts, another opens within a most surprising way." He said that maybe there's a great and wonderful adventure awaiting us in the tropical land we're planning to see soon. We're both getting excited about it—starting to count the weeks, and soon the days.

My "kitchen of dreams" looks empty and bare, and the other rooms as well. Everything's been carefully packed away in the old mill with the help of Matthew's family and Enos and Betty and their youngsters. We got our dinner at the Millers', taking the cocker Spaniel pup along for the boys; Captain goes to Matthew's younger brother until we come back.

Now, in less than an hour, we'll be starting for Pennsylvania along with a vanload of other travelers. All we need to take is our clothes and a few accessories, so we're traveling light. We're thankful that the roads are good for traveling, and that no major blizzards are predicted in the near future. Even Jocelyn and Ken came over to say good-bye, and on Sunday afternoon our church district had a farewell hymn singing at Owen Hershbergers. I'm going to miss them all so much—what if I get a terrible case of *Heemweh* (homesickness)? We were presented with a gift of a beautiful comforter consisting of a lot of different and unique patches, each one made by one of our friends, with their name embroidered on it. It's a lovely keepsake, but we don't expect to be able to use it in Belize so we'll take it along to show to Mamm, Daed, Sadie, and the boys, and put it in storage there until we get back.

Golden Gem for Today:
Trust is a beautiful, rare Christian grace.
It never comes until it is led on by its sisters
Faith and Charity. It makes the spirit
very bright and peaceful.

February 26

It's good to be home with my dear, familiar family. Yesterday the whole clan of friends and relatives were here for dinner. Today Mamm put a quilt into the frame, and Priscilla and girls, Barbianne, and Grandma Annie were here to quilt. I'll have to soak up these memories, for I'm afraid it will be a long time until I see them all again.

Matthew and I went tobogganing again on Grandpa Dave's hill, took long moonlight strolls along the creek, and even went skating once.

Sadie and I were able to have many a sisterly chat once again, and plan to write to each other at least once a week after we're in Belize.

Tomorrow we plan to get together again to make doughnuts and potato chips, and then spend a few days visiting old friends in the community. Matthew is helping Peter and Crist in the woodworking shop tonight, and Mamm, Sadie, and I plan to spend the evening quilting and having some time to visit by ourselves.

Tomorrow, Matthew and I will look up Mrs. Worthington and Clark to renew old acquaintances there. Pamela Styer is taking us over, so we'll be able to visit with her, too. It seems we have everything planned down to the last detail, every minute jam packed with worthwhile things to do before we leave. It's hard to believe that in just over a week we'll be on our way to far away Belize. It's coming closer and closer, and having put our hands to the plow there's no turning back, no chance to come flying home to Mamm right away if it's not what we thought it would be. But we trust it will be a worthwhile and rewarding experience.

February 28
.... Our visit with Mrs. Worthington and Clark was a worthwhile one, and just as we thought, her gift was a generous one! We now have our visas and passports and have booked passage on a huge passenger ship traveling from the New York harbor to the coasts of Belize. Matthew chose that method of transportation over traveling by van because it's something he has never done before. He says we'll come home through Mexico then. Pamela Styer will take us out to the harbor, and Peter and Sadie will go along to see us off. It's too bad that Matthew's family can't be there, too. Oh, how will we ever be able to do without seeing our families for perhaps a whole year? I just can't imagine it.

We will have traveling companions—a Mr. and Mrs. Yoder who are going to do some volunteer service in another part of Belize.

That's so much nicer than if we'd be traveling alone. I haven't much time to write tonight, for it's late and we're starting out early tomorrow morning to do some more visiting.

March 5

....

Here we are, on board this huge passenger ship just off the New York harbor, headed for Belize! Matthew has gone to take a tour of the ship. I've chosen to stay here on this deck chair until I get used to the rolling feeling of the ship. It all seems like a dream—after watching the shoreline disappear, being surrounded by the ocean on all sides with the sparkling brilliance of the sun shining on the water. Feeling the gentle rolling, seeing the endless whitecaps, the crying sea gulls, and we even saw a school of what looked like porpoises. The ocean in the distance looks exactly like a hill, or even a mountain we must climb. I'm hoping we won't run into a hurricane and get seasick, for Mrs. Yoder has already gone down and curled up in her bunk, half queasy in spite of having swallowed a double dose of seasick pills. It's still hard to believe we actually are here now, on this voyage, with so much to see and learn. A cool brisk breeze is blowing up now, and the whitecaps are sparkling like millions of lustrous jewels as far as the eye can see. It's really awesome. "Great and marvelous are your works, Lord God Almighty; just and true are thy ways, thou King of saints" (Revelation 15:3).

Innisfree Orphanage

This is Saturday evening—already three weeks have passed since my last diary entry. It's a pity I don't have more time to write about this enchanting land and its people, where howling blizzards and frigid north winds are unheard of. Uncle Cephas and Aunt Barbara Bontrager, both in their late fifties, met us at the harbor, and there we parted company with the Yoders. Cephas had hired a taxi, and what a thrilling ride that was through the city. Wow! It seemed like everyone drove in the middle of the road and didn't even pretend to yield an inch for oncoming traffic until the very last minute. They all seemed to drive like maniacs, with a constant tooting of the horns and frequent swerving and dodging for pigs and livestock on the road being taken to market. On the outskirts of the city we stopped at a stand for some mangos and were fascinated by two monkeys swinging from a tree, chattering raucously, almost as if they were angry with us for disturbing their peace.

Cephas explained that they must be the family's pets, for monkeys swinging from trees so close to the city are not at all a common sight. It was a very long trip and there were some breathtaking, hairpin turns as we got out into the country, and of course, there were no guardrails except some big rocks. Then the gravel road wound through brush country, citrus groves (no choice Amish farmland in sight), and grassland. Once, as we careened around a turn, there was a speeding Land Rover headed our way. He seemed to be aiming directly for us. Our driver swung to the side, and the Land Rover passed with only a few inches to spare. So it was with a sigh of relief that we pulled up to the Spanish-style building with a sign in front that said "Innisfree Orphanage." Barbara told us that the people who started this orphanage years ago gave it that name after the Lake Isle of Innisfree in Ireland, a symbol of remote rural harmony and peace.

Time for evening devotions—maybe tomorrow I can write more about the orphanage and our living quarters.

March 27
.... Today we attended our first church services here in this settlement called Pleasant Valley. It was a very small group of only five families. Several families were away on a trip, and they tell me that two of those families (and possibly more) are thinking of moving to Paraguay in the near future, so I don't know what will become of this struggling little group. The weather was very warm,

and it feels good to sit on the rocker and relax. Matthew and I plan to take a walk tonight when it's cooler to see more of the countryside. We have a small apartment here at the south end of the orphanage, about the size of the *Daadi* (grandparent) end at Mahlon Swartzentrubers—a small kitchenette, *Sitzschtubb* (sitting room), and bedroom. There are cheery curtains at the windows and colorful homemade touches here and there like a sofa cover, a crocheted afghan on the rocker, and a flower garden quilt on the bed, which was the work of two Amish girls who lived here before us.

Barbara is a white-haired but youthful faced, bustling, motherly type woman, with a touch of warmth and a sense of humor twinkling out of her eyes. Cephas is the solid, dependable, level headed type, and I think they make a very good set of foster parents. It wonders me why they never had any children of their own. Maybe sometime she'll tell me.

March 28

I am sitting here by the open window. It's a beautiful, peaceful evening with birds singing and the air sweetly scented with dewy, tropical breezes. I marvel at the charm and beauty of the mountains in the distance—the mountains that seem to both of us to separate us from our loved ones back home. Is that a sign that we have *Heemweh* (homesickness)? I don't think so, even though home tugs at our heartstrings. There's so much to do and see and to learn.

The mountains are often so shrouded in clouds that the view to the summit is dim and hazy, and it makes them look blue through the mists. I think of them as intriguing and enchanting, but probably if I could see into some of the homes of its inhabitants—the shabby, slab wood huts, the poverty and crime, the superstition and hostility, the stealing and drunkenness, I wouldn't think them so enchanting anymore.

This morning Matthew and I fed and milked the four cows—it will be our job from now on, but in the morning only—and also fed the dry cow. The sun was just peeping over the horizon, the roosters were crowing, the birds were chirping and singing, and it all seemed so homelike. It was almost like we could hitch up Cephas' horse to the buggy and just drive a few miles through the gap in the mountains and be able to visit either Matthew's family or mine on the other side!

Golden Gem for Today:
Faith is the eye of the soul which sees the unseen.
It is the power within us which realizes,
or makes real to us the great eternal things
of the other world. But oh, how little is there
within us of the clear, bright triumphant faith
which makes these things real to the soul, and
finds in them life and peace and safety.

The children here at the orphanage are adorable, but I wish there'd be a few babies to hold and cuddle. Aunt Barbara said that the babies are the most sought after to be adopted into families. When a baby does come in, it is often soon chosen by a couple that wish to adopt it.

My work here so far has been doing laundry, cooking and baking, and cleaning and mending, although I do help to give the little ones their baths in the evening. They are getting over their shyness toward me, and it warms the heart as they start to trust and accept you. This morning while Matthew and I were out in the shed, peacefully milking the cows, we heard a great racket outside, coming closer fast. We rushed outside in time to see a whole group of boys and a few men running past yelling, "Mad dog! Mad dog!" It gave me the shivers. I didn't see the dog, so I don't know if they were chasing the dog, or if it was chasing them, but apparently the dog ran under the foundation of a shed, and the boys threw rocks underneath until it slunk out, and then one of the men shot it. They made a great ceremony of burying the dead dog, as if it was a great sport. Uncle Cephas later said that it is often a question of whether or not the dog really is rabid, for it is great sport to the boys when the cry, "Mad dog!" goes up.

Matthew and I went for a walk tonight to see more of the countryside, but I found myself at first fearfully eyeing the brush and bushes, half expecting a mad dog to jump out any minute. But when the peaceful, dusky darkness began to fall and a breeze heavy with tropical scents wafted over us, I forgot about it and enjoyed the charm and intrigue of twilight in a mystical land. The sound of singing floated up to us from down in the valley, and somebody was strumming on a guitar. The orphanage children were outside frolicking on the lawn, and the sound of their wholesome laughter and shouts while playing sounded just like the children back home, even though some of it was in Spanish.

Cephas and Barbara sat on the porch relaxing after their day's work, and we joined them there when we got back. We visited until the children came trooping in, tired and ready for their baths and bedtime Bible stories.

March 30
.... Matthew and I went for a drive tonight. We hitched Molly, the small driving mare, to the cart and went "in style." I didn't need to watch the bushes for mad dogs lurking behind them tonight!

We passed a pathetic looking hut that seemed like it could tumble over any minute, it was so tottery. There were old cornstalks set up around it, probably to cover the cracks in the walls, and the roof was patched with cardboard. I had to wonder how they would fare when it rained heavily. But that wasn't the worst of it—there was a big mud hole right in front of the doorway, and several huge pigs were wallowing in it. Flies were everywhere, and I'm sure that we stared and stared. One of the sows wandered inside the house, and a little girl of about five years hit it with a stick and yelled at it, trying to drive it out. As it ran out, it bumped against the doorframe, shaking the house so that we held our breaths in fear that the whole thing would collapse and come tumbling down. A woman came walking up from the creek carrying two buckets full of water, and a well-aimed kick from her sent the pig wandering away, but not very far. The one in the waterhole grunted and rumbled ominously, and was left unmolested. When we came back, we told Aunt Barbara about it. She said that the little girl is one of six young children that the mother is trying to keep fed and clothed by herself. The water they use is parasite infested, and the children are often sick. It's enough to give one the shudders. I wonder if I'll be able to sleep tonight. There is such a big difference between the rich and the poor in this land; not too very far from here there are several very stately mansions that probably have all the modern conveniences available.

There goes the bell—so I must go help the little ones with their baths and bedtime stories.

March 31

Barbara got to talking and reminiscing about the old days today while we were preparing dinner. The first few years were dim here. There were a lot more snakes around then, although most of them weren't poisonous. They had a very good dog though, and in the first few months that they were here he killed around a dozen snakes. One morning they were awakened by the dog's racket in the field just outside their bedroom window. He was barking into the thickets and Cephas quickly got his gun and went outside. Sure enough, there was a big snake in the underbrush, and a poisonous one, too! Before Cephas could aim and fire, the dog made a dive for it, intending to grab it behind the head and bite and shake it to death as he usually did. But this snake was too quick or too big or something—anyway, it managed to bite the dog first. Cephas quickly shot the snake, then went to the dog's aid. He grabbed a chicken that was wandering in the yard, killed it, and put some of the fresh, warm chicken meat on the dog's snakebite. (This, he had learned from the natives, was the best remedy for drawing out the snake's poison.) The chicken meat turned green with the poison, and he quickly replaced it with another piece. The dog eventually recovered, but he was sick for awhile and walked slowly and stiffly. They didn't give much for his chances of recovery there for awhile.

And then another time they actually had a snake in the house! Barbara said that Cephas was the only one who saw it, and he didn't tell her about it until a few years afterward. She was bathing Johann, who was a baby then, and Cephas went into their bedroom for something. The room was dimly lit with a kerosene lamp, and in the dimness he thought he saw a curled up rope on the rug. He turned up the wick of the lamp, and horror of horrors, saw that it was a huge snake! Without thinking, he grabbed both ends of the rug and tossed it right out the window. One of the children had pushed it open without a screen earlier, and that was where the snake had come in. He quickly went outside with the gun, but when he came around the corner of the house the dog had already killed the snake, which was not a poisonous one. Barbara said she was thankful that Cephas didn't tell her, for she's sure she wouldn't have been able to sleep in peace for many a night and would've had nightmares often. I'm certainly glad that the snake population has been reduced around here and that we have good screens!

Golden Gem for Today:
Oh Savior, humble our wills until they bow,
like Thine own, in perfect submission
to our Heavenly Father's will.

April 1

Nurse Cassandra, who is a tall, angular woman with gray hair pulled tightly back into a bun, was here today to give some of the children their immunization shots, and she stayed for supper. Somehow or other, we got around to telling about Cephas' snake story, and she said she's more afraid of mice than of snakes. Imagine that! She'd rather wake up to seeing a snake on the rug beside her bed than a mouse! Another amazing thing she said is that she's more afraid of thunderstorms than of earthquakes! I guess what she's more used to is less frightening to her. She's an interesting, talkative woman, and has all kinds of pep. She's been a big help to Cephas and Barbara here in the orphanage over the years, and doesn't charge for her services here. She's also a midwife and delivers lots of babies.

She had a scary story to tell. Not long ago she was spending the night at the home of friends, and in the middle of the night a burglar swinging a heavy machete attacked the front door with blows and shouts, commanding them to open the door. At first they weren't too alarmed, figuring he was probably staggering drunk, but when he became more and more violent and brandished a loaded revolver, they were really worried! He finally did leave though, shouting back threats and shooting (they didn't know what he was aiming for, as they didn't find any bullet holes). It sure gives one the shivers. That was only twelve miles from here. But Cassandra didn't seem to be bothered about it and went right on telling stories in her jolly way.

We had fresh strawberries for supper, and they were sure delicious with shortcake and milk. I guess we could make the folks back home jealous, for they'll have to wait another six to eight weeks for their berries to be ripe.

Today's date, April 1st, brings back memories of

Enos and Betty Miller's children, how they loved to play tricks on each other and then shout "First of April!" Back home the robins will be starting to sweetly sing, while here I saw a bunch of green parrots, a reminder of how far from home we are. Nurse Cassandra took us for a ride tonight in her Jeep, and we saw more of this land of mystery and intrigue that lies in the shadow of the mist-blue mountains.

April 2
For the past few days we'd been quite puzzled over what was causing the sudden drop in the cows' milk production. They were giving only half as much milk as they did at first, and Cephas and Barbara couldn't understand it either. I think maybe they were beginning to think we're greenhorns and not milking the cows dry, but then last night something happened to shed some light on the subject. It was around midnight that I awoke to find Matthew dressed and ready to go out with his flashlight to check on the dry cow, who was about to freshen. I got a notion to go along, so I dressed quickly and grabbed a flashlight, too.

The stars were twinkling by the millions from the sky above, and the moon was shining just like it does back home. The air was warm and balmy, and far off in the hills faint strains of music floated on the breezes. The tropical night scents made us feel like taking a longer walk.

Inside the barn we found the cow doing fine and

about to give birth, so we decided to stay and witness the miracle. Suddenly we were startled to hear stealthy footsteps outside, and the barn door latch rattling slightly. We quickly snapped off our flashlights and hid behind the two big feed barrels. The door creaked open and a shadowy figure cautiously sneaked in, carrying a lighted candle and a bucket. It was a woman with a kerchief tied on her head. She quickly squatted down by the first cow and began to squirt the milk into her pail. Soon she moved on to the next cow and when her bucket was full, she set it outside the barn door and brought in an empty pail. She filled that with milk from the other two cows, then left as quietly as she had come. After she had carefully closed the barn door, we went to the window and watched her extinguish her candle and put it into her pocket. Then, carrying the heavy burden of two pails of milk, she quickly made her way down the road. The mystery was solved. We're both sure it was the same woman we saw carrying pails of water to the ramshackle little house where the pigs wallowed in the mud hole outside the door. Poor woman. I'm sure she has a hard life, trying to feed and clothe all her children without a husband's help. We stayed with the cow until her fine, healthy-looking heifer calf was born. This morning when we told Cephas and Barbara about the milk thief, they were amazed at her boldness. They decided to confront the woman and ask her not to steal again, but to come over in the morning and they would give her the milk. They help out the poor whenever they have anything to spare from the donations for the orphanage. They will just have to put their cheese making on hold for awhile.

It seems that in this land those who are mired in poverty, like this woman, have almost no way of helping themselves out of it. They're the victims of circumstances and even though she'd work her fingers to the bone, she couldn't rise above it. I am sure that she gets no happiness from her life of sin (if such is the case) and probably has no awareness of sin. It is sad, but not uncommon for this country.

April 3
....
There were no church services today, so Matthew and I decided to hitch up Molly and go for a long, leisurely drive to see more of the countryside. Just as we were about to start off, little Hester came running and wanted to go along. Cephas gave his permission and lifted her up to sit between us. She is around six years old but small for her age—a little live wire! Such big, inquisitive eyes, sometimes alight with mischief and daring, and sometimes bright with merriment.

The mountains weren't so mist-blue today as the weather was very clear, and they seemed closer and more beautiful than I ever saw them before as we started off on our drive. Too often we get so absorbed in our work and daily cares that we don't take the time to notice and appreciate the beauties of nature—God's handiwork. We saw birds and wildflowers and nice trees, and seeing it all through the eyes of a child, a delighted little girl, made it seem all the grander. On the down side, we passed a little wooden hut with no windows in it and just an opening for a door. Two children chased each other around their home, and Hester suddenly got a notion she wanted to join them, too, and jumped off the cart. So we tied Molly to a tree, and a friendly looking man came out of the hut and talked to us. He invited us to come in and we were shocked at how poor their living conditions were. Bits of sky showed through the slab wood roof and we could imagine what the condition of the dirt floor would be when it rained. There were only two small rooms in the hut, and soon an elderly lady wearing a long skirt came out of the other room and gave us a toothless smile—something we see so much of in this land. I suppose their teeth rot away and then they must do without. The man said that his wife died in childbirth. Now his mother lives with them and takes care of the children. We visited for awhile, while Hester played happily with the little boy and girl, then started for home again.

Tonight Barbara invited the church families over to sing. We sat on benches in the yard and the sweet, age-old hymns seemed to float down over the valley in the calm evening air and echo back to us. As singing usually does, it gave us a feeling of gladness and well-being. When it was nearly dark, a caravan of donkeys loaded with baskets and other burdens driven by two moustached natives passed by, reminding us again that we were far from home in a strange land of contrasts.

Hester came and sat on my lap. The night birds twittered sleepily and the evening breezes brought peaceful, tropical scents and sounds up from the valley. She fell asleep before long and Matthew carried her in to her bed.

Golden Gem for Today:

My child, I know thy sins and thy unworthiness
better than thou knowest them thyself.
Yet again I bid thee come. If thou hadst no sin,
wherefore did I die for thee?

April 4

I find that working for Barbara is a joy and a blessing, for she is very kind-hearted and never gets out of patience. She is a good foster mother to the youngsters here and they all seem to love her. I did the laundry today and when I put their folded laundry away into her room, I saw a nice little poem I wanted to copy fastened to the heart-shaped pincushion on her dresser. I asked her for permission to copy it, and of course she said yes.
Here it is:

When God looked down upon the earth
And chose to put new blessing here—
Gifts from above
To show His love
And lighten earthly joy and care.
He gave the sky the sunset glow,

Gave fragrance to the lily's blow,
To children he gave play,
And then to every yearning soul
He gave a gift of tenderest worth—
A mother.
                    —*Author unknown*

These children would probably never have known a mother's love if Barbara hadn't been willing to give her all for them, and to give them the needed nurturing and care. I hope that if I ever am a mother, I can be just like her.

April 5
.... Tonight there was one of those breathtaking tropical sunsets, with the enchanting, dusky, velvety twilight settling over the countryside and a coppery moon rising up over the yonder mountain. Matthew and I went for a walk again tonight in the cool of the evening. Looking at the moon, we wondered if our families at home were able to see this same moon at the same time we did, and Matthew thought they could, which made them seem a lot closer for some reason. We both claim to have escaped *Heemweh* (homesickness), for there's so much to do and see and learn here. Today was the first day we actually worked with the children and they are mostly, but not all, little brown Indian children of the Mayo tribe, and as cute as can be. I'm eager to get to know all of them by face and by name.

Barbara told me that when they first took the position as manager for this orphanage they hired local help for a few months. There were two native women helping here, but then after awhile things began to disappear. The women claimed to be very much puzzled. At first it was just food, then dishes and cookware began to disappear, too. This went on until even the kerosene cook stove was carried off, and the native women themselves never came back. I guess they had what they wanted. Cephas explained that there is so much alcoholism in these parts, especially among the men. With that, there is no one to provide for the women and children who live in abject poverty. Their houses are often not much more than mud huts. I've heard say that half the world doesn't know how the other half lives. Do we remember to give thanks enough for the blessings we have and the heritage handed down to us by our forefathers?

April 6
.... Tonight a little baby boy was brought into the orphanage; he had been found abandoned in an old kiln. He was dirty, wet, and shivering, even though it wasn't cold, and his lips were blue. It was a heartbreaking sight, but we soon had him bathed, fed, and in clean clothes. He was peacefully sleeping after awhile.

I found a poem attached to the wall near the mirror in the dispensary that someone gave to Barbara.

I'll copy it here:

> You dear little lost boy, with eyes of brown
> Were brought to us, ragged and hungry and
>   down,
> No blanket around you, you were shivering
>   in the rain;
> Sick and neglected, your eyes filled with
>   pain.
> We'll feed you and give you our tenderest
>   love.
> We'll rock you to sleep like the angels above,
> God sent you to us, and bids us his love to
>   share;
> Dear, little lost baby, angel unaware.
> —*Author unknown*

April 12
.... On Friday night
Matthew and I went for a stroll along the old dirt
road that leads past the canal. We were about to turn
back when we heard a faint whinnying from the high
grasses among the trees. We went to investigate and
could hardly believe our eyes—it was a real live colt
(not just a mirage) and he didn't run away when we
approached him. We soon saw why. His hind foot
was wedged between two chunks of rock and he was
trapped! He was a yearling, thin and gaunt, and he
was wild-eyed with fear. When Matthew tried to free
him, he lunged about, whinnying shrilly. But

Matthew continued to talk softly and soothingly to him. Soon he stopped trembling and began to eye us with more curiosity than fear. Matthew ran back to get a halter and neck rope. He soon had the colt freed and led him up to the barn. He must not have been trapped long, for he was still frisky and capered about, several times nearly getting away from Matthew. He had probably been running loose in the wilds for some time already, judging by his leanness and all the burrs in his coat.

Then yesterday we found out that four weeks ago a yearling colt was stolen from a ranch ten miles away and was never seen again. We sent word to the owner and tonight he came down. By this time, Matthew rather wanted the colt for here on the farm, and so Cephas made an offer and the ranch owner agreed to sell. Matthew will begin his training early and try to make a fine horse out of him—the colt has good breeding. And it will give Matthew a taste of his old job on the horse farm. The colt is dark brown with a white star on his forehead, two white hind feet, and excellent confirmation.

I'm having an enjoyable time too, with the little Indian baby that was brought in a week ago. He could hardly be taken for the same child anymore. He's looking so much better and more filled out. He is more active, too. He smiles and coos and loves to be rocked and cuddled, just like the babies back home. We named him Pablos, which one of the girls here at the orphanage picked out for him. I think I would've chosen the name Teddy, for he reminds me of a little brown teddy bear, except he's sweeter and cuddlier.

The mist-blue mountains are hazy with clouds again tonight, hiding the summit. Whenever I happen to glance up at them, I am reminded of the verses, "I will lift mine eyes unto the hills, from whence cometh my help, my help cometh from the Lord, which made Heaven and earth."

April 16

Not having been blessed with children of their own, Cephas and Barbara take in these homeless waifs as their family—they are Mama and Papa to the children even though none of them are adopted. Their living quarters are at the north end of the orphanage and are much more spacious than ours. Cephas manages a large farm and Matthew is now his *Gnecht* (hired man). I'm thinking I can finally tell the children apart. (I was about to write kids, but remembered just in time that Barbara won't have them called that—she says baby goats are kids, not children.) At one time there were three times as many children than there are now, but just now they are Radonna, Orlando, Johann, Eduardo, Hester, Nadina, Octavia, Maria, Jovalina, Yolinda, Verlynde, Santos, Rosita, Ninette, and Pablo the baby that was just brought in. There goes the bell. That must be Nurse Cassandra, come for the weekly lice check, so I'd better go to help.

I'm feeling some twinges of homesickness tonight, in spite of my best intentions not to succumb to it. It is mostly for the lovely springtime season we're missing there, I think. Matthew feels it, too. He even misses the clip clop of the big workhorses (the native horses here are much smaller) and all the friendly Holstein cows' contented moos as they file out into the meadow after milking. By now the trees along the creek will be budding, the robins sweetly singing and starting to build nests. The meadow grass will be growing greener, more lush, and coming out in buttercups. The breezes will be fresh and fragrant. We missed the hyacinths, daffodils, and tulips blooming. The old apple trees will soon be covered with pink, fragrant blossoms, and the cherry trees covered with their white, shining veils. I had a letter from Sadie today— maybe that was what brought my homesickness on. She wrote that out in the cozy old barn where the pigeons coo from the rafters, there are several new litters of baby kittens and a new baby colt, and a brand new set of twin calves. All are adorably wobbly, but healthy. She had been copying poems out of Mamm's book of prose and poetry and found a copy of a prayer of St. Francis of Assisi. She decided to send it to me, for she thinks it very fitting for our work here in the orphanage. I agree, it is something to strive for, and will copy it here:

CHANNELS OF HIS LOVE

Lord, make me a channel of Thy peace
That where there is hatred—I may bring love,
That where there is wrong—I may bring
    the spirit of forgiveness,
That where there is discord—I may bring
    harmony,
That where there is error—-I may bring truth,
That where there is doubt—I may bring faith.
That where there is despair—I may bring hope,
That where there are shadows—I may bring
    light,
That where there is sadness—I may bring joy.

Lord, grant that I may seek rather to
    comfort—than to be comforted,
To understand—than to be understood
To love—than to be loved.
For 'tis by giving that one receives,
It is by self-forgetting that one finds,
It is by forgiving—that one is forgiven;
It is by dying that one awakens to eternal life.

April 30
....

                        This morning I was
up quite early to give Baby Pablos his morning bottle—one of my favorite tasks since he is here. I keep
dreaming of somehow or other devising a way of
taking him along when we leave here next spring.

Matthew and I could adopt him, this little dark-eyed, brown-skinned Indian baby. But, having one of our own by then would be even better. I was sailing in a dream boat on the clouds of fantasy when I heard a sharp rap on the door, then a grating voice saying, "Hello, hello, Pleased to meet ya!"

"Was in de Welt?" (What in the world?)

I didn't know whether I should go get Cephas, or first take Pablos and run back to Matthew, but the voice kept on saying, "Hello! Hello!" Finally, I gingerly opened the door a crack and the first thing I saw was the unblinking gaze of a parrot! A blue, yellow, and green parrot, with a hooked, yellowish beak and brilliant wing feathers. He was on a perch in a rusty old cage, carried by Marcinda, a girl we met down by the irrigation canal. Her eyes sparkled as she said, "Here's a gift for you. Her name is Polly, and she will say everything you teach her to say." She set the cage on the porch and was gone even before I could have said, "No, thank you." I didn't know what Cephas and Barbara would say, and I didn't have long to wait to find out. They were not too thrilled, to say the least. "Just another mouth to feed," Cephas said, pretending to be exasperated, and Barbara said, "Oh dear, what do we want with a noisy, loud-mouthed bird around?" The children, though, were absolutely delighted. Time will tell whether or not the big bird will be allowed to stay at Innisfree Orphanage. It's still out on the porch and has been saying, "Hello! Hello!" and "Buenos dias!" to all who pass by. Apparently it can talk both

Spanish and English, and maybe if it stays, we can teach it Pennsylvania Dutch, too.

May 5
.... Matthew and I were invited to our closest Spanish neighbors for supper. Ramon and Carmine Gonzalas are a charming, well-to-do couple in their mid-forties. They have a beautiful home on top of a hill with quite a view across the valley. I'm always astounded at the big difference between the rich and the poor in this land. There was just one flaw to the evening—our lack of appreciation for Carmine's excellent cooking. We had to leave the table, our eyes watering and mouths burning. I wonder how long it would take to get used to these hot, spicy foods, and if we'd ever prefer them over the bland fare we are used to.

May 13
.... I got a fat pack from home today—a chatty, sisterly letter from Sadie; short, but welcome letters from Daed, Peter, and Crist; and a long letter filled with motherly advice from Mamm. They all brought tears to my eyes and momentary pangs of *Heemweh* (homesickness). Mammi had ended her letter with a few well-known lines on selfless love: "Love is patient, and kind, love is not jealous nor boastful, it is not arrogant or rude. Love does not insist on its own way, it

is not irritable or resentful, it does not rejoice at wrong, but rejoices in the right. Love bears all things, believes all things, hopes all things, endures all things. Love never ends" (1 Corinthians 13).

She concluded with these lines: "Love always rejoices in the best efforts of another and does not fix its attention on flaws. A mother does not berate her child for stumbling when he is learning to walk. A kindergarten teacher does not scold her pupil when her crayon strays outside the picture when she is learning to color. A person who is quick to see the mote in the eye of a fellow Christian and displays a critical attitude has a lack of fervent charity."

I suppose she felt it would be helpful to me in my work with the children here. Mama and Papa, as Matthew and I have started to call Cephas and Barbara behind their backs like the children do, are perfect examples of having the right kind of love for these homeless little waifs in their care.

May 15

Is this the warmest time of the year here? Whew! Tonight when it was nearly dark, Matthew and I went for a walk down to the irrigation canal in the valley to cool off. We haven't seen any snakes yet, but we'll be on the look-out for them. We've been told that there are some poisonous snakes in the area, although they are not plentiful. We're both trying our best to master the Spanish language so we regale each other with phrases like *buenos dias* (good day) and *muchas gracias* (thank you) and *ayudanze por favor* (help me please), etc.

Tonight as we dangled our feet in the water, the young Spanish girl who brought the parrot to the orphanage joined us again (Marcinda). She knows quite a bit of English, and with the bit of Spanish we knew we were able to communicate. She has snapping dark eyes and round, rosy cheeks. She is a very friendly girl. I'm hoping to get to know her better.

Golden Gem for Today:
If thou but touchest the hem of My garment,
thou shalt be made whole.

May 17
....
A letter arrived today for Barbara and Cephas from Mary and Martha of Ohio, the two girls that worked here in the orphanage before we came. Barbara gave the letter to me to read. Mary wrote: "We do miss the children so much, but admit that many times we felt like the old woman who lived in a shoe and had so many children that she didn't know what to do." Martha sent a poem that sums up her feelings:

Oft times my thoughts have gone wandering
Back to that intriguing land
Where children oft homeless and hungry
Find shelter and a kind, loving hand.
They came, some tattered and ragged

And some without shoes on their feet.
We give them our love, and at bedtime
Tuck them in with a kiss so sweet.
—*Author unknown*

I know this place is called an orphanage, but at least half of the children are not orphans: they have mothers and fathers who cannot or will not support and care for them. How sad.

May 20

We have some extra help here at the orphanage these days. A few days ago, Marcinda came and offered her help—she says she doesn't look for any wages and is a willing worker. She has gotten Polly the parrot to say quite a few more phrases, and we others are all trying to teach her something new, too. On the same day that Marcinda came, Juan, a young Italian, came to Papa out in the garden, swinging a machete, and offered to clear off the one-fourth acre lot down the road which belongs to the orphanage for the sum of forty dollars in U.S. money. So Papa gave him the job, and when I passed today on an errand he was really swinging that machete and was nearly done. He has the blackest hair I ever saw and a black curled mustache. I wonder if he is related to Marcinda. He never comes in for meals, but Marcinda takes food out for him, and at dusk they go off together.

....
Reports have just reached us that hurricane-like winds have struck Belize City near the coast, causing flooding of the Belize River and homelessness for quite a few. I suppose it's nothing compared to the hurricane they had in 1961. That one caused so much destruction that they moved the capital of Belize inland to Belmopan. About half the citizens of Belize are Roman Catholics, I am told, and some of them celebrate holidays by partying a lot, even during Holy Week, which is the week they celebrate the crucifixion of Christ. The name of this country used to be British Honduras, but after the country gained its independence in 1973 it was renamed Belize. It's a nice place to live, but naturally we are looking forward to going home and having a place of our own.

July 23
....
Whew! Did we ever have a scare last night! Matthew and I were writing letters home until about ten o'clock, then he blew out the lamp and we crawled into bed. It seemed like I had been sleeping for only a few minutes when we were awakened by terrified screams from the children's rooms. We grabbed flashlights and rushed over, finding the room's only window open and the children too terrified to speak at first, all except little Ninnette, who kept saying, "Bad man, bad man," and pointing to the window. By that time Papa had come

over from his room, and upon investigating outside, found footprints and scuffed grass beneath the window, which led out to the road. Someone (a bad man?) must've been at the window, either looking in or trying to climb in. It gives me the shivers still. Papa did not seem too very worried—he thinks it was probably just a hungry boy thinking it was the pantry window and wanting to snitch a few bites. But he left instructions to make sure that all windows are locked after this, and the shutters closed.

August 1

Today brought us a letter from Matthew's sister Rosabeth. She is to be the Birch Hollow school teacher next term, and I hope she will have time to write of many interesting experiences as teacher. It makes me feel homesick for them all, Matthew's big happy family at home in Minnesota. I'm beginning to wonder, will we ever have a family of our own?

Rosabeth also wrote of a happening in their community—one of her best friends at the singings has been the target of unkind slandering. She mentioned neither names nor details, but wrote, "Let us not stoop to unkind gossip or mud slinging, but instead take a good look at ourselves and all our hidden soul stains. Let only those without sinful flaws hurl stones of condemnation, and may we others steal quietly away in the condemnation of our own conscience and leave the erring one alone with the

Savior." I had to smile—how typical this attitude is of Rosabeth. I can't imagine her throwing stones or repeating unkind gossip or writing nasty unsigned letters.

August 4

Nurse Cassandra invited me to go along in her Jeep to make a house call. We visited little Anastasia, a schoolgirl who has rheumatic fever. I was surprised at the poor condition of their home. It was just a little hut with thin walls, and the little girl rested on a mat on the ground floor. If these people could see our big, sturdy farmhouses back home, would they think we are living a rich man's life compared to them? Anastasia had a bright, friendly smile for us and took her medicine without complaint. Her mother was a pleasant looking woman and their home was clean. I had to wonder if there was a dad in the picture, or if he had up and left, like so many fathers in this land.

On the way home, driving along a winding gravel road with tall grasses on either side, Nurse Cassandra suddenly slammed on the brakes. In front of the Jeep, in the middle of the road, was a slithering green snake. Nurse Cassandra claimed that it was a very deadly and poisonous one. We grabbed rocks and soon had reduced it to a pulp. Matthew and I have often talked about climbing mountains and camping out in the enchanting mountain land, but now it would take a little something to persuade me to go. I wouldn't have enough spunk, even though it has been over thirty years now since the first Amish and Mennonites moved into this country, and I have never heard of anyone being killed by a poisonous snake. But I think camping out would be asking for trouble.

Golden Gem for Today:
Thy prayers and thy sacraments will not be accepted for thy warmth and favor, but for My merits and sacrifice.

September 7

.... Ever since that scare we had two weeks ago when the children were frightened in the night and the window was left open, we've been extra careful to make sure no one can get in. There are shutters on every window now (or so we thought), and we try to always remember to close them every night. Well, last night after midnight we heard Polly, who was in a cage on the porch, loudly screaming, "Hello! Hello! Buenos dias! Buenos dias!" over and over. I could tell that she was really excited about something, for she usually never talks at night. So Matthew and I dressed and went to investigate. We heard running footsteps down the hall and the outer door banged shut. Polly was now hollering, "Pleased to meet ya!" over and over, when suddenly she stopped in mid-sentence, squawked loudly, then all was quiet. Papa was up in short order and together we looked in on the children and found them safe and sound asleep. We found Polly with the doormat thrown over her cage and her head tucked under her wing. She has proven herself an excellent watchdog and has gone up several notches in Papa's estimation. She has earned her keep.

After searching for awhile, we found where the prowler came in—a window in the closet that had only a screen tacked over the outside of it instead of a shutter. The screen had been cut and the window noiselessly pushed open. It gives me an eerie feeling, and Matthew too feels that it's more than a hungry boy hoping to raid the pantry. Maybe Cephas is more worried about it then he lets on; he probably just didn't want us to be frightened.

October 2
....

Matthew seems to be perfectly happy here in this "land of enchantment," as someone once called it. He likes his job of farming the acreage for Cephas and loves the little Indian children as well as I do. But still, there is that longing to have one of our own.

October is here already, the lovely month of crisp cool weather that we are missing back home. We won't be there to enjoy it—the leaves on the trees along the creeks turning bright and colorful in reds and golds, and contrasting with the browns and greens of other leaves already dead or not yet changed. Harvest time, the bright blue skies, the first frost, mounds of apples and pumpkins, wild geese winging their way southward, and tangy fresh cider made from sweet, juicy, Red Delicious and Russet apples. It's time to stop daydreaming, for here comes Matthew, carrying little Pablos on his shoulder. He sure likes children, and what a good daddy he would make.

November 12

Today is our "no church" Sunday and Barbara gave me a stack of reading material for Matthew and me to choose from. There was "Light from Heaven," "Paula," "The Waldenesian," "Touching Incidents," "Search to Belong" (which Matthew began to read), and "Genevieve, or God Does Not Forsake His Own." I had already read all the others, so I read "Genevieve." It's such a very old-fashioned, but meaningful story. I was so impressed by Genevieve's piety and her Christ-likeness that I'm going to copy the main parts of her story here in my journal. The book is very, very old, its pages are loose and about to fall out, and I'm afraid it's been out of print for years already and the story may be lost and forgotten eventually. It is truly an account of how God does not forsake his own, even though it may appear so and be difficult to trust in his grace. Matthew has fallen asleep so I think I'll copy it now. I think I'll be able to have it done before it's time to help with the suppertime duties.

Genevieve, Or God Does Not Forsake His Own

Genevieve, who lived hundreds of years ago, was the wife of Count Seigfrid of the Pfalz. Because she was good and kind and delighted in taking gifts to even the poorest and lowest in the country, everyone in the whole earldom loved her. One day Seigfrid was sent away to battle, and he instructed his servant Golo, whom he thought to be trustworthy, to rule his earldom and take care of Genevieve while he was gone. But Golo was a scoundrel, and in Seigfrid's absence dared the virtuous Genevieve to commit sin, asking her to forsake the count and take him, Golo, for her husband. When Genevieve refused and ordered him to leave, he became angry and had Genevieve put into the castle prison, in a damp, dark room reserved for the worst criminals. He then sent a messenger to Count Seigfrid, telling him that his wife was guilty of great wickedness. Genevieve was entirely innocent and prayed that her husband might not believe the lie. But Seigfrid, upon receiving the message, was so angry that he ordered his faithless wife to be put to death.

After several months in the dungeon, Genevieve gave birth to a baby boy, which she named Dolar. She had no cradle nor pillow for him, so she wrapped him in her apron, pressed him to her heart, and wept.

When the executioners came to take Genevieve to the middle of the forest to be executed, she pled for her and the baby's life, promising them that if they would let her live, she would stay hidden in the densest part of the forest with her baby and never go back until they came for her. Finally they agreed to it, and took her into a wild and lonely part of the woods.

It was hard for Genevieve to still believe in God's love for her in her abandonment, but now, trusting him, she would find out how God would provide for her and her baby. She found shelter in a cave, which, unknown to her, was a hind's home. When the hind (a female deer) came back into the cave where Genevieve and the baby were, she was quite tame. Her own young one had been killed by a wolf and Genevieve was able to nourish herself and the baby with the hind's milk. Its warm body took the place of a stove in the cave.

Back at the castle, Genevieve had left a letter for Seigfrid with a servant girl and instructed her to give it to him upon his return from the battle. When Seigfrid came home and found out how Golo had deceived him and of Genevieve's innocence, his great sorrow bordered on insanity, and he wept violently. He cursed his hasty temper that had caused him to so rashly condemn Genevieve without waiting to hear her explanation.

For seven years, Genevieve and Dolar stayed in the wilderness, nourished by the hind and edible roots and berries. The child, Dolar, developed into a fine, healthy child. Genevieve taught him about the Heavenly Father who cared for them, and to do good.

Then one day, as Count Seigfrid was hunting in the dense part of the woods, a hind ran by him. He sent an arrow after it but missed, so he followed it on foot. It disappeared into a cave. Seigfrid entered the cave and found his wife, whom he had thought to be dead. There was a joyous reunion, and tears of both remorse and joy were shed upon finding his wife and son alive. He ordered a sedan chair to have Genevieve carried home, and followed with Dolar. Behind them came the faithful hind, who followed them to the castle. Seigfrid had a special stable built for the hind, and during the daytime it would run loose, often going up the castle steps to Genevieve's door, not leaving until she came and petted her.

Genevieve did not live to be old, and when she died the hind lay down on her grave and would not rise again nor eat. In a few days the faithful animal, too, was dead.

Count Seigfrid erected a beautiful monument for Genevieve's grave, at the foot of which, cut out of stone, lay a hind.

The End

Oh, there goes the gong, calling me to help with supper, and I'm just done with copying the story.

November 14

Marcinda has been coming to help faithfully every day, but Juan hasn't come back to ask for work since he finished clearing the field. Marcinda and I take turns doing the kitchen work, cleaning, laundry, and caring for the children (the best part!).

We found a scrap of prose in a drawer that either Mary or Martha, the former workers, must have left. It summed up our feelings as well. They wrote: "We love them (the children), laugh with them, play with them, kiss away their little hurts, end their fights, give them rides on the swings, rock them, spoil them, and each one will be a precious memory to tuck away and remember after we're back home again."

After we're back home again—to me they are like five magic words! But I'm not complaining, as this is a very meaningful time indeed.

November 16

This evening Papa hitched Molly, his small driving mare, to the cart for us, and Marcinda and I went for a drive out to the citrus grove on the hill, a distance of about two miles. It was a lovely evening, a bit cooler with a refreshing breeze blowing. On the way home Marcinda told me a bit more about her home life—Juan is her brother and he has left to find a job on the seacoast. They had been living with her widowed aunt, but she remarried recently, and they felt it was time to move out. Papa and Mama have given their consent for Marcinda to live at the orphanage. We do need help, and she's a good natured, decent girl. I invited her to attend our church services on Sunday and she readily agreed.

Marcinda wanted to drive on the way back, and I had just given her the reins, when, with a wild yell, some dirt clods came flying out of the rustling, swaying, tall grasses on either side of the road, hitting Molly and forcing her into a gallop. We saw the tops of several tousled heads among the grasses, so it was probably just some mischievous little boys. It reminds me of something that Sadie wrote in her last letter—a few young people back home were returning from a singing, when their horse was shot at with a BB gun, which nearly caused the horse to bolt and run. That would've been nearly as exciting as having the carriage catch fire!

Golden Gem for Today:
Thy heart, thy mind, thine affections, thy motives, thy will, thy life, all must be brought under the power of God.

November 17

I think Hester, who is six years old, must be the liveliest and most inter-

esting little person at the orphanage. Today Mama and Papa went visiting and Marcinda and I were left to pilot the boat. It was Hester's job to feed the chickens. There are only a few dozen broilers in the wire chicken yard out back, and she had just entered the pen when out of the corner of her eye she saw a big, fierce-looking (or so she thought) rooster stalking her, ready to attack. She swung her bucket of feed at him and hit him squarely on the head. Plop! Down he fell, still as death, and Hester came running to the house, yelling at the top of her lungs, her eyes big and frightened.

"I killed the big rooster!" she shouted. "I didn't mean to do it!" She began to cry loudly and Polly the parrot added to the din by yelling, "Thief, thief! Catch the thief!" Marcinda jumped up from feeding Pablos, deposited him in the playpen, and said, "I'll put the tea kettle on the stove for hot water. We'll have a scrumptious fried rooster supper." She went outside with Hester to see the dead rooster, and when she came back in she said, "Yep, the rooster sure is dead."

When the water was boiling, I carried it out to the pen, with Hester behind me, and lo and behold, before our very eyes the rooster came back to life and jumped up! After staggering around a bit, he began to peck and scratch around in the ground for bugs as if nothing had happened. Seeing the astonished look on Hester's face, I couldn't keep from laughing. Polly was yelling, "Traitor, traitor, hang the traitor!"

Solemnly, and without a smile, Hester said, "Next time I'll throw harder."

November 24

How fast this first two years of our marriage have flown! Most of the couples who married when we did are parents by now, and it makes my heart ache that we are not. Oh well, here at the orphanage we are surrounded by babies of all sizes to love and cuddle. But still, no one can blame us for wanting one of our own. I said something about it to Nurse Cassandra and she just can't believe that a person my age could be worried already.

"Enjoy your freedom while you have it," she said blithely. "All too soon you'll probably be tied down." Doesn't she know that that's what I want?

November 26, Thanksgiving Day

We won't have any roast turkey with stuffing and mashed potatoes and cranberry relish for dinner, but we do have so very much to be thankful for. May we remember to give thanks to the Giver of all good gifts, and never take our blessings for granted. Matthew wants to take the time to read the story of Genevieve this afternoon. He became interested in it after I told him parts of the story.

He thinks that Count Seigfrid must've been a real cad to judge and sentence his dear wife without giving her a fair trial and no chance to explain the situation. He must've had a hasty, fiery temper and probably regretted it immediately after it was too late to recall the messenger. *Ya well*, I must go help with breakfast.

December 1

....

The last month of the year, and I'm beginning to long for cold, snow, ice skating, and sledding. Christmas won't seem like Christmas here in this tropical climate, I'm afraid. Marcinda seems glad for the privilege of living here at the orphanage and is not afraid of hard work, even though it's all volunteer work. She adds sparkle and cheer to our days and makes the endless, repetitious tasks seem fun. She gave me a homemade card today, I suppose for Christmas, even though it said nothing about Christ's birth. It was flower-bordered, with a hand-drawn bird and a nice verse penciled on. She and I are fast becoming good friends, which is a blessing. There are no Amish girls near my age in this group and no other young married couples. I would have been very lonely without another girl to talk to.

December 21

....

As I sit here on the porch in the cooler twilight, I hear the sweet sad strains of a haunting melody from somewhere down in the valley and far across the countryside. I can see a man with a pair of oxen working on a hillside. Matthew is unhitching the horses (they are a far cry from the beautiful, stately Belgians at home, but they serve the purpose). It's hard to believe that Christmas is so close, with the weather so unlike December in this tropical country. Mamm sent a letter—back home the *Yunge* (youth) are skating and sledding and having taffy pulls and the women are having quilting parties and comfort knottings and everyone is getting the butchering done and having cookie exchanges.

My thoughts stray out to Minnesota, too, to Rosabeth and her job as Birch Hollow schoolmarm. Is she having a Christmas program this year? I can just picture all those bright, eager faces singing the Christmas carols and reciting their poems. But we have no lack of bright and eager young faces right here at the orphanage, so there's no need to get *Heemweh* (homesickness). Mamm sent me a plaque with the following etched on:

CHILDREN LEARN WHAT THEY LIVE

If a child lives with tolerance
    He learns to be patient.
If a child lives with encouragement
    He learns confidence.
If a child lives with praise
    He learns to appreciate.
If a child lives with fairness
    He learns justice.
If a child lives with security
    He learns to have faith.
If a child lives with approval
    He learns to like himself.
If a child lives with acceptance and friendship
    He learns to find love in the world.

There are plenty of opportunities here at the orphanage to put this advice to use and with God's help, I want to do so.

What a day. I feel too drained to write, but I must. Barbara is a loving, motherly sort of person, and I think she loves each one of her motherless children as if they were her own. Cephas too, is a good natured and kindhearted loving dad to them. Imagine their consternation this morning when they woke up to find that six-year-old Freddy was gone. No one heard any noises, but apparently, because we had no prowlers for such a long time, somebody got careless and left the shutter open to the boys' bedroom window. There was a set of large footprints outside the window, and Freddy's small ones beside them. Papa said sadly, "I guess Polly failed us as a watchdog this time. Come to think of it, it's strange that we haven't heard a squeak out of her this morning yet."

Radonna ran out to the front porch to check on her and came back with tear-filled eyes. Polly was gone, too. No time was wasted in notifying the police and sending for help to organize a search party, but now it's evening and there are no clues as to his whereabouts. Freddy is small for his age and of Italian descent, very dark-haired. Just yesterday he went with Matthew and me to the store on the cart with Molly the mare. He chattered brightly and was full of questions, and when we were nearly home he asked, "Did you know that my dad will come for me soon? He promised."

My heart ached for him, for on his records it says that his dad was killed two years ago. Who then could it have been that snatched the little boy out of his sleep? We hope and pray that he will be kept safe from all harm and be speedily returned to us.

"Like as a father pitieth his children, the Lord pitieth them that fear him. For he knoweth our frame; he remembereth that we are dust" (Psalm 103:13-14).

December 25
....
It hasn't seemed like a very joyous Christmas, with Freddy still missing and a fine, misty drizzle coming down all day. Marcinda and I have been using our spare time these past weeks to make homemade gifts for the children: yarn dolls on a string, crocheted items, and other small crafts. It seems strange that no mittens, caps, boots, and scarves are needed in this land—no firewood must be chopped, no coal hauled. But I never realized I'd miss the invigorating cold and scenic snow-covered countryside so much. The Christmas story and the carols are the same, though, no matter what the climate. From Luke 2: "And she brought forth her firstborn son and wrapped him in swaddling clothes and laid him in a manger because there was no room for them in the inn. And there were in the same country shepherds abiding in the field,

keeping watch over their flocks by night. And, lo, the angel of the Lord came upon them, and the glory of the Lord shone round about them: and they were sore afraid. And the angel said unto them, Fear not: for, behold, I bring you good tidings of great joy, which shall be to all people."

December 26
.... Marcinda attended our church services these last few times, even though she probably couldn't understand more than a few words of the sermon. We ought to have an interpreter for her. We've been so glad for her help here in the orphanage these days, what with Mama nearly driven to distraction about Freddy. If only we'd know that he is alive and well and in good hands. Papa drove Molly to the store this afternoon. He said there's a rumor out that someone saw Freddy with a man hurrying down a city street, but he couldn't get to the bottom of it— who it was that saw him, and where.

January 12
.... Nurse Cassandra has asked if Matthew and I could accompany her on a week-long trip giving immunization shots and health-check care to various villages. Knowing Matthew, I knew our answer would be "yes." Nurse wouldn't have asked us if Lynford and Lora Lehman, distant relatives of Barbara's, had not

arrived here at the orphanage looking for work for an indefinite length of time.

We start already tomorrow morning at daybreak, so I'll have to pack my satchel tonight. Cassandra said it will be a long journey up into the hills, stopping at various towns along the way, hopefully arriving at our sleeping place at bedtime if we don't have too many flat tires (or meet up with too many snakes). Her brother has a cabin up in the mountains, and we have permission to use it. She claims it will be worth the climb up there (the last part of the journey being on foot), as he is quite a wealthy man and owns his own helicopter. He is away just now, though, so we'll have the cabin to ourselves. I think I'll pack my journal, as there should be a few interesting happenings to relate along the way. I'm sure it will be better than sleeping in a barn, sharing quarters with a cow and a steer as Cephas and Barbara once did.

Time for bed, for tomorrow morning it will be BON VOYAGE!

January 13
.... Whew! This was a long, tiring, but interesting day. If I close my eyes I can see lines of somber, brown-eyed children (Mayan Indian) patiently waiting for their shots and whatever treatment was needed. We stopped at four different villages, or rather, the last place wasn't really a village, just a small hamlet on the hillside. It was quite a hike up to the cabin. Cassandra calls it a cabin,

but Matthew and I call it a palace. It feels like we're in the lap of luxury! We have thick, luxurious sleeping bags to sleep in, and it's real cozy in here with a steady downpour outside drumming on the roof. Soon after we arrived it seemed like the very heavens opened with a downpour, flashing lightning, and beating rain and wind. We're so glad it waited to start until after we got here. I suppose tomorrow we'll have to contend with the much talked about sticky Central American mud. At the last place we stopped, a kind-hearted peasant woman insisted on giving us supper, and a delicious one it was. She served us sandwiches made of cassava flour bread instead of the usual tortillas, and a hot, spicy dish I have no name for, but we liked it. Could it be that we are getting used to these seasonings already? But the best part of the meal was oxtail soup. That was something that Mamm used to make years ago. Matthew liked it, too, so I asked her for the recipe and she gave it gladly. I'll copy it in my journal here, so I don't lose it:

OXTAIL SOUP

Cook one oxtail or soup bone in a heavy kettle with just enough water so that it can be browned.
Pour off the fat if there is some.
Add water, salt to taste.
Add 1 tablespoon rice per person.
Cook for 1½-2 hours.
Add water as needed.

When nearly ready to serve: Take 1 egg, put in a bowl and beat for a few minutes. Then add a little water, a tablespoon or so of flour, and drop into soup by the spoonful. Cook another 5 minutes or more. Ready to eat. Delicious.

She also passed around a big bowl of papayas, oranges, bananas, and mangos, and even sent some with us for breakfast.

Ya well, Matthew is dozing in the big stuffed recliner, so it must be time for bed. Nurse Cassandra is still watching TV.

Listen to that wind. Brrr! It sounds like wintry winds, but it's actually a tropical storm. Let's hope this palace is solidly built.

January 14
.... We haven't ventured outside our cozy palace all day; the storm is too wild. We decided it must be a hurricane, even though it's not hurricane season. Tonight we heard some weird, spine-chilling screams coming from the jungle. Could it be a big gorilla or baboon? We sat there as if frozen, staring wide-eyed at each other. Cassandra, sensing that the ordeal was getting to be nerve wracking, got down the Bible and read to us from Psalm 23. She read, "The Lord is my shepherd, I shall not want, He maketh me to lie down in green pastures, he leadeth me beside the still waters. He

restoreth my soul: he leadeth me in the paths of righteousness for his name's sake. Yea though I walk. . . ." She stopped there suddenly, for we again heard the shrill scream, this time closer to the cabin. She finished her verse then, rather weakly. Trying to sound cheerful, she said it was time to hit the sack and that we shouldn't worry, as we are safe here. (She is scared too, but doesn't want to frighten us more.)

January 15
.... We slept fitfully and sometime during the night I awoke to hear a roaring sound, like the rushing of mighty waters down over the mountainside. I drifted off to sleep again, and in the morning we discovered that the mountain stream had turned into a rushing river. (We must not be as near to the top as we thought.) The rain was still pouring down heavily at times, and every now and then we heard some ominous rumblings. Cassandra made no secret of the fact that she was worried (scared to death, as she herself put it). There is always the danger of a landslide, or mud-slide in this case, and then a person, or even a whole village, could be trapped or even buried alive. It's not pleasant to think about.

Venturing outside in the storm was out of the question, so Cassandra and I spent the forenoon cleaning the cabin from top to bottom, even though it wasn't all that necessary. There is plenty of food in the cabinets, enough to last us for a week if necessary. Matthew is keeping busy in the woodworking shop in the basement, trusting that the owner won't begrudge him the use of the tools and wood. I keep thinking of the man who built his house on the sand and when the storms came and the winds blew, the fall of it was great. I just hope Cassandra's brother built on a solid foundation—those dark, deep rumblings are truly frightening and the rain is still coming down. It makes me think of the words of the song, "On Christ the solid Rock I stand, all other ground is sinking sand."

January 16

Sunshine at last this morning! A welcome sight after more downpours last night. We threw open the windows to let the fresh air and sunshine in—and a few minutes later there was a fluttering of wings, and a cry of "Buenos dias! Buenos dias!" A familiar looking parrot alighted on the windowsill. We all cried, "Polly!" at the same time, and there was no doubt about it, that's who it was! She seemed to be really glad to see us, and took turns perching on our shoulders and softly and affectionately saying, "Pleased to meet you," over and over. It's hard telling what hardships she may have endured since we saw her last. Apparently she had a dry place to stay while it rained so hard, for her feathers were dry.

We packed up our satchels, planning to make our

way down the mountainside to the Jeep, when Cassandra suddenly exclaimed, "Oh look, a note!" Sure enough, attached to Polly's leg, close to her feathers and fastened with a string, was a small scrap of white fabric with the words, "Ave Maria, Help, Help!" printed on it.

"Looks like someone needs help fast," Cassandra said briskly. "We'd better go see." We had gone only a few steps down the path when already our shoes were clogged with sticky mud. It was slow traveling, and when we reached the plateau we were dismayed to find that there had indeed been a landslide. A thick avalanche of mud covered everything and blocked our path as far as we could see.

"We're trapped!" Cassandra cried, turning to Matthew with anguish in her eyes. "What shall we do? What if my Jeep is buried in the mud?"

"Yes, and what about the person who wrote that note?" Matthew wondered. "What if he was buried alive?" We all shuddered, hoping he was still someplace on the mountain. If only we could find him. So we retraced our steps and made a thorough search of the area. We were about ready to return to the cabin when a stone whizzed past us, then another flew by. Polly came sailing down from the branch of a tree just as a third stone came flying, and it hit Polly on the wing. She fell to the ground, whimpering pitifully. Cassandra sprang to pick her up, and at that moment I spied a small figure peeping out from behind a tree. "Why, it's Freddy!" I cried in amazement. At the sound of his name the little boy came out from his hiding place, every bit as wide-eyed with astonishment as we. When we called his name, he walked slowly toward us, then broke into a run after recognizing us. He was overjoyed to see us, but when he saw what he had done to Polly he began to cry, and would not be comforted until Cassandra had fashioned a splint for the broken wing out of her first-aid kit and fastened it with tape.

After we cooked breakfast for the half-starved little boy and he was fed, bit by bit we got the story of what had happened to him since he was kidnapped from the orphanage. He claims his dad came for him one night and took him along. Could it really have been his dad if the records say he died two years ago? Freddy is certain it was, and he claims they were living in a hut in the mountains (he and his dad and Polly) until it rained so much that their hut collapsed and they crawled into an animal den to keep dry. His dad attached that note to Polly's leg and released her, or sent her off. He then fashioned a sort of raft out of several logs on the creek bank and launched it into dangerous, turbulent waters to go for help. So, there's a ray of hope that help might come from that source. The phone lines are dead and the radio's dead, so we're staking our hopes on his dad reaching his destination. Tonight after dark we again heard the weird, shrill, primitive scream—but far off. Freddy is delighted with sleeping in this luxurious cabin, and so are we, mighty thankful for safe shelter from the storm.

.... Another day spent
thus on the mountaintop. We've been debating about
whether it would be wise to start traveling across the
other side of the mountain in order to reach civilization on that side. Cassandra has no idea how many
miles it would be or whether it would be safe.
Matthew thinks there's too much danger of more
mudslides, and I keep thinking of poisonous snakes,
angry jaguars, and other possible dangers. The
mountain vegetation is dense, about like a jungle, and
I think we ought to see cute little chattering monkeys
swinging from the trees and eating bananas or a tall
giraffe or a herd of elephants. Matthew says that is
Africa, this is Central America. *Ya well*, I can always
imagine, and there are monkeys here.

Tonight after dark we were badly frightened by
that shrill scream again, real close to the cabin. It's an
indescribably spine-tingling sound when it's so
close. Luckily Freddy was sleeping already. Matthew
has now finished making a lovely cabinet, ready for
staining. I hope Cassandra's brother doesn't mind
his using the tools and generator.

.... Since we're stranded up here, my thoughts travel homeward a lot to
Mamm and Daed, Peter, Sadie and Crist, Priscilla and
family, and all the other dear ones back home. I guess
I'm feeling the *Heemweh* (homesickness) more since

we're stranded up here. Will I ever really see them all again and our old home place by the creek? In the spring, the creaking windmill, the birds singing sweetly and joyously, a peach-colored sunrise sending its rays over a field of new mown hay, releasing its wondrously sweet scent, the lush green meadows full of yellow dew-washed buttercups, the fragrant blooming lilac bush by the lane, the contented cows wandering peacefully down the cow path after the milking, planting the garden seeds in the soft dark earth while a robin joyously serenades us, planting petunias, geraniums, and marigolds. Then in the summer, gathering fresh, wholesome garden goodies, the first long-awaited sweet corn on the cob, going boating, peaceful sunsets, August lilies, sitting on the porch and visiting with the family in the evening after the work is done. Then in autumn, the leaves turning color, watching the antics of playful squirrels as they scamper in tall, acorn laden trees, housecleaning, raking leaves, drying apples. Then in winter, cold and snow, skating and sledding, the laughter of merry children, Christmas cheer. There are so many things that no income value could ever be compared to. The best things in life cannot be bought with money. The joy and satisfaction in gifts, such as the beauty of the countryside and the change in seasons, are ours to be enjoyed if we have peace with God and are living within his will. I hope I never again take such blessings for granted. Why does it so often go until we realize we might lose something that we can really fully appreciate its value?

.... Matthew keeps himself busy in the woodworking shop with Freddy at his side, and it seems to me that they are very glad for each other's company. Cassandra has told me some of her life's story. She has gone through a lot of hardships already as her dad was a drunkard. She shed some tears as she related several incidents—in fact, we cried together at the sad parts. When her dad came home drunk they would all, including her mother, run outside and hide in the woods until he was sober again. Almost every evening he would go to a tavern and then come home close to morning, staggering drunk. If they failed to hear him in time and weren't able to run out, he would be dangerous and violent. Oh my, those poor children. They were innocent. There is a lot of sadness and suffering in this world brought on by sin.

She said that the next day, when he was sober again, he would feel very bad about what he had done and declare that he would never touch another drop of liquor again. But each evening he would yield to the temptation of, "Just one more time. Just one more time, and then I'll stop." He went on like this day after day until he began to suffer from delirium tremens. His whole family prayed continually for him, that he might be delivered from Satan's clutches before it was too late. One day, as he yielded once more to temptation and was turning in at the saloon, he felt a hand on his shoulder, pulling him back. He was so astounded that he went home and stayed sober. The next day his craving was so bad that he again headed for the saloon and again he felt a hand pulling him back. This happened a few more times, until he finally repented and was delivered from the power of Satan. It's a remarkable story, but Cassandra claims that it is true. He then became a Christian and never drank again. That's one case of a sad story that had a good ending.

January 20
.... Well, it appears that Matthew and Freddy haven't been spending as much time in the woodworking shop as I thought, for without saying a word about it to us, Matthew built a good, solid raft big enough to hold us all. He is still very dubious about the whole thing and feels responsible for us. He will leave the decision about whether or not we should attempt an escape by raft up to Cassandra. She said she wants to sleep over it, as we people would say. There certainly are dangers involved, but neither do we want to stay here always. Wouldn't it be too good to be true if Cassandra's brother would come to rescue us with his helicopter? It would be my preference, for even though I wouldn't admit it to Matthew, I'm awfully afraid to get on that raft.

Cassandra opted to try the raft, and so yesterday morning (was it really only yesterday) we gathered at the creek's bank with our satchels, prepared to launch the raft. Matthew had made two long sweeps to guide us, if it was possible. We were encouraged by the fact that the creek had calmed down considerably and was no longer a raging river torrent, but still, we had no idea of what dangers lay around the next bend—rapids or waterfalls or deceptive currents. Matthew had fashioned handholds for us on the raft, and clutching our satchels, we climbed aboard. Taking the plunge, we pushed off into the current. I'm sure we all sent prayers heavenward, for the raft began to tremble and shudder, and then we were off. The banks and trees were flying by, and the raft pitched and churned for awhile as it gathered speed. Once the raft plunged and began to spin and we held on for dear life, but in a moment it straightened out again, and I willed myself to relax. I could tell that Cassandra was scared to death, as I was, but Freddy loved it when we hit turbulence. Matthew looked grim and determined, and I knew this was no fun for him either, for if we should perish in these waters he would feel it was his fault.

Once, before we even had time to prepare for it, we were cast into a rock strewn area where the water seemed to turn violent, and the raft twisted and bucked so that it was a wonder we all managed to hold on. Then, abruptly, the water plunged down through a steep, narrow canyon much too narrow for the raft.

Matthew swiftly and expertly guided us to shore with the sweeps. We scrambled down over the rocks, carefully maneuvering the raft down with us. Then, in the calmer water, we launched into the deep again. There in the middle, the current was still swift and the force of it nearly upset us, and the raft plunged and jarred mercilessly for a while. Behind us the spray from the waterfall rose high into the air and a maze of mist hung over it. It was all so breathtaking and awesome, and if only we hadn't been so scared it would've been quite a thrill. I had to wonder how Freddy's dad fared going down the river while the water was even more violent. We were speeding onward with the current, and once we sped around a curve in the creek so swiftly that the raft tilted crazily and foam spray nearly obscured our sight, then next it was a deep calm pool where we could catch our breath and relax. After that, the creek's current seemed to be much slower, and we soon discovered why—the creek bed was widening. Calmer waters were the rule now rather than the exception, and our outlook brightened considerably. Then there was a shout of joy from Cassandra—she was the first to spy signs of civilization, and very soon we drew alongside a small village. Matthew, with the sweeps, guided us to shore, and oh what a joy it was to be on solid ground again. With such gratitude and thanksgiving we went ashore! Matthew built a fire on the bank for us to dry our damp clothes a bit, and we had a small picnic with the provisions we brought along.

Time to go—I'll finish this account of our adventure later.

Here we are, at home at the orphanage at last! It seemed like a long, weary journey, in an old rattletrap truck with half of the windshield missing, the axles tied with baler twine and wire, and the doors loose and rattling, yet the driver drove like a maniac! We saw a lot more of Belize, bustling and modern on one side, and poverty and superstition on the other. There is such a wide rift between the rich and the poor, with thinly veiled hostility often between them. For those mired in poverty there isn't much they can do about it, which is the discouraging part. If only those rich landowners who have invested in thousands of acres of land were willing to share—somehow or other. We saw huts made of cornstalks and cardboard, sticks and slabwood, shabby and tottering. Nurse Cassandra said the poor people are often malnourished, living on tortillas and black beans, and many of the children die before they reach school age, weakened from a combination of malnutrition and respiratory diseases coupled with childhood diseases. These people are trapped in a never-ending cycle of poverty, superstition, drunkenness, and illiteracy, and no amount of hard work can lift them from it. There have been uprisings and murders in the remote regions; terrorists and guerillas find them good hiding places while trying to recruit soldiers for their armies. It's a grim picture that dampens my joy of being at home again. I hug the little babies, many of whom are descendants of the Mayan Indians that have inhabited the southern part of the country ever since the sixteenth century, and think that I want to do all that I can to help them.

Golden Gem for Today:
We cannot come fitly to God without godly sorrow for our past sins, and a steadfast purpose to lead a new life.

January 30

I was helping Nurse Cassandra today in her office and found it very interesting and enjoyable. She has several posters hanging on the wall. One says, "A BABY IS GOD'S WAY OF GIVING US HOPE FOR TOMORROW," and another one says, "A BABY IS GOD'S OPINION THAT THE WORLD SHOULD GO ON." I wonder, will we ever have a baby of our own to love? Cassandra has gotten her Jeep back unharmed. A large sheet of tin and a sturdy tree apparently had protected it. Her brother brought it back for her.

February 5

It has been good to be back home again these past few weeks and in the routine of work here at the Innisfree Orphanage. Lynford and Lora now say they plan to stay on for a year, taking over our duties here since Matthew and I had not planned on staying longer than a year. I was secretly cherishing hopes of returning home before too long, but now Matthew is all enthused about something else. And he has enthusiasm enough for both of us. Those families that had been intending to move to Paraguay have found a closer place they intend to call home in a few months—a place called Kolancho Summit. The elevation is higher than here, resulting in a cooler climate that is more favorable for growing fruit trees, berries, and other crops similar to those we raise back home. So now, in a few days, Matthew intends to start off on another pilgrimage to see the new settlement these families are hoping to start. I just hope they don't meet up with any poisonous coral snakes, unscrupulous campesinos, dangerous Brahman bulls, or other dangers. What if Matthew likes the new settlement so much that he wants to stay? The truth is, I am beginning to fall in love with this country too, and maybe if we'd go home now I'd get so much *Heemweh* (homesickness) that we'd have to turn right around and come back.

February 6

Great news for Marcinda! Freddy's dad showed up here at the orphanage and they were joyously reunited. He had his arm in a cast and his forehead still bandaged. Apparently his raft ride down the raging river was a good bit rougher than ours was! The amazing part is that when Marcinda saw him she turned white as a sheet and her hand flew to her throat. Could it really be possible that this was her dad? She had always been told that her dad had died, and there he was, standing before her in person. Bit by bit they pieced the scraps together, and this is how it was.

When Marcinda was eleven, her mother became ill and she and Juan were sent to live with an aunt. Later they were told that their mother had died, but were never told about baby Freddy. Her dad had someone take the baby to the orphanage, telling them that both his parents were dead, apparently figuring that they wouldn't take him if they knew his dad was alive. Later Marcinda and Juan were told that their dad had died, too. Now she is reunited with her dad and little brother. The reason his dad kidnapped Freddy was because of the lie he had told, fearing they would refuse to give him the boy. Well, if I know Mama and Papa right, he will have to prove himself as a real dad who can provide a proper home before they let Freddy go. Marcinda plans to stay on at the orphanage as before. Oh my, the days will seem long and lonely here with Matthew gone, and I suppose keeping busy will be the chief antidote.

February 7
.... We said our tearful (on my part anyway) good-byes, and I watched until the taxi with the four men in it disappeared out of sight around a bend in the road. Let's hope that Kolancho Summit is not an area where there are poi-

sonous snakes. Just yesterday I heard a rumor that there are, in some areas, tiny poisonous snakes nick-named "yellow beards." They are reported to be so poisonous that if one of them bites you, you have less than fifteen seconds to live. The only hope of saving your life is to use a machete to quickly cut off the limb where you were bitten. Whew! It gives me the shivers. But nobody around here seems to know whether it really is true or just a rumor. And then, just last night there was a report of terrorists attack-ing a missionary couple. That supposedly happened a couple hundred miles from here, but still, it's too close for comfort.

February 8

What wouldn't I give to have Matthew safely back! Apparently the word was spread among the natives that the men folk are all gone in our group, with only a few women here to guard our homes and possessions. Last night at about midnight, the stillness of the night was shattered by the hysterical squawking of Polly the parrot (our good watchdog has been returned to her post). Then we heard loud knocking on the door, until the whole house seemed to vibrate. Then there was shouting, and banging on the shut-ters demanding for us to open, RIGHT NOW! Of course, we did no such thing. We were trembling like leaves in the wind after being awakened out of peaceful slumber by such a racket. Papa told us to ignore them, while we did all we could to comfort the crying children. Not finding an entrance, the burglars finally gave up and left, but this morning we heard they were much more persistent at other places, pretending they were armed and demanding money and saying they would not leave until their night's work was worthwhile to them. I'm feeling quite low this morning, for besides the dismaying feeling caused by the thieves last night, I'm also contending with a flu bug of some sort. I just hope Matthew hasn't caught it, for it sure would spoil his trip. I'm praying it's not *Gale Sucht* (hepatitis), for that has been making its rounds lately and is hard to get rid of. Mama has told me to stay in bed, and I'll gladly obey. Marcinda has just brought me a cup of bancha tea, bless her.

February 9

Nurse Cassandra was just here and she said I have to stay in bed for a week. She is not sure what is wrong—oh dear, I hope it's not malaria or some other tropical disease. I am so captivated by Grandmother Bontrager's diary that I think I'll either read it all even though my head aches, or read just a part of it everyday until Matthew gets back. Marcinda was just in with a bouquet of wild flowers and a cheery visit. She says she is sure that is all that's wrong with me is "missing Matthew," and that the minute he comes back I will be okay again. I know better.

.... Marcinda is a good nurse—bringing me tea and fluffing up my pillows. Her visits never fail to bring me cheer.

I've been reading a little from the history of our people, the Anabaptists. It's really something to think about how our forefathers endured many hardships in the pursuing of religious freedom and the settling of new frontiers, both when they came across the ocean to America, and those that later followed the trails westward. In Europe there was the threat of war and persecution, hostile governments, and lack of freedom of religion. In 1544, Menno Simons wrote to a fellow Christian: "We preach, as much as is possible, both by day and by night, in houses and in fields, in forests and wastes, hither and yon, at home or abroad, in prisons and in dungeons, in water and in fire, on the scaffold and on the wheel, before lords and princes, through mouth and pen, with possessions and blood, and with life and death." His name became connected with the Anabaptist movement and his followers paid a high price in following their convictions. But they were sincere, willing to suffer, even die, for the truth they had found. Many were tortured for their faith, but they refused to recant; many were burned at the stake and put to death in other ways. It said in my book that Menno Simons encouraged his remaining followers to work the land, milk cows, and avoid urban life. Many of them have done so.

Time to sleep again. Tomorrow it will be a week

since I last saw Matthew. It makes me wonder how they are making out on their trip. Will they like the lay of the land in Kolancho Summit?

February 14
.... Cephas brought the mail from town and there was a fat pack of letters from Owen and Lizzie Hershberger and children. What fun I had reading them, even though I shed a few tears of homesickness.

Valentine's Day. Marcinda and Lora are planning a Valentine party for the children this afternoon when Mama and Papa will be away. They made heart shaped cookies and candy.

February 15
.... I had a welcome letter from Matthew today. He plans to be home in a week or so. It sounds like he is real enthused about the area and wishes I would be along. He didn't write many details, so I guess I'll just have to wait until he comes home to hear more. It's good he doesn't know I haven't been well, he'd probably worry needlessly and it would spoil his trip.

At last Nurse Cassandra gave me permission to be out of bed and up and around, but says I must take it easy for a week—do nothing but eat and sleep. She has not diagnosed this mysterious malady yet, except she says possibly mono. But then, she's not a real doctor either. I'm just so very thankful that I'm recuperating.

February 20
....

Today I had baby Pablos once again, and he (temporarily) filled an empty spot in my heart—or maybe I should call it an ache. Santos, Rosita, and Ninette were with me, too, and I told them stories and helped them to look at the books they brought me. They're so sweet and adorable. Pablos is just learning to walk now, and it looks so cute to see him toddling around on his sturdy little legs. I'm counting the days (or hours) now until Matthew gets home—I can hardly wait to hear what he has to say. What if he comes home and says he bought a farm (or ranch or plantation—whatever they call it here)? I guess I'd better not think about it too much.

February 21
....

We have had word from the travelers! One of the men called up the bulk food store and told them to give us the message that they will be gone a few days longer than planned, but that they should be home sometime this week.

They are pleased with the farms there and need more time. It's so hard to be patient for yet another week. Oh well, as long as they come home safe and sound none of us will complain. We haven't had any more trouble with burglars or trespassers, for which we are very thankful. We've heard that a new set of law enforcement officials are coming into office, and that crime will soon be much less here in Belize. Let's hope that it is true!

Ya well, my time's up for writing. I am going on kitchen duty once again today for the first time since I was laid up. I am so very thankful that I am well again—I guess we'll never know for sure what it was that I had. I know one thing, that it had nothing to do with what Marcinda keeps teasing me about. She says that I was just missing Matthew. Of course I missed him, but that wasn't what made me sick. She just loves to tease!

February 24
.... The men are home! Matthew is home. There are no words to express my thankfulness. He came home yesterday at supper-time and had many glowing reports of the land and ranches they saw. We stayed up late, talking and talking. All of the men who traveled with him signed papers to buy, and Matthew rented (yes, rented) a farm for a year. He wouldn't have done it without consulting me, but one of the other men urged him to, saying that if I'm not interested he will rent the

farm himself instead and farm it along with his. Matthew says it is a scenic farm similar to the ones back home, with a dairy set up on it, just like we are used to, except there are brown Swiss cows that go with the deal instead of Holsteins. The plastered house is about the size of the farmhouses back home and in real good shape. A winding creek flows through the property. There is a four-foot high stone wall, about a foot thick, surrounding the buildings and property. The big barn and outbuildings are neatly painted, and there is a grove of timber in back of the buildings. The owner of the farm said he hasn't seen a poisonous snake on his property for years. There are no scrub oak and brush areas, nor weeds nor high grasses, and that would make a big difference. The farms that the other men bought are similar. The enthusiasm is high and even I have forgotten my longing to go "back home." Surely I can make it here for another year on such a picturesque farm.

March 1

We are planning to move to our farm in two weeks, and I'm sure I won't have time to write anything but current happenings for quite awhile. So much has happened to us here that we would never experience at "home." Maybe someday I'll put my journal into story form! Maybe our children will want to read it someday, if we ever have children.

I remember Grandma Annie saying she does not

like stories—only true accounts. She used to say in that emphatic way of hers, "Stories are a bunch of lies—that's what!" Oh well, I remember Matthew's dad once said there is nothing wrong with fiction stories if they're uplifting and the author labels them as fiction and doesn't try to pass them off as true.

Now to get back to our moving—we'll have to go shopping for some furniture. I think longingly of my beautiful handmade furniture in storage at home and my clock, but we'll try to not get more then we really need for just a year. Not all of the rooms will be furnished. I am getting to be as excited as Matthew about moving, even though I'll miss the children here terribly. After all, we've waited for over a year to have a home of our own again. I think I'll write to Mamm and Daed to see if they couldn't somehow or other come down to visit us in the near future. That would be too good to be true.

Golden Gem for Today:
I am the Light of the world. If I go before thee,
there shall always be light on thy path.

March 10
.... At last I've summoned up the courage to have a heart-to-heart talk with Mama Barbara, something I wanted to be sure and do before we leave here. They have been childless all these years and I've often wondered about it, but never dared ask. She told me that when they

were married for fifteen years they finally gave up hoping that God would ever send them a child. That was when they came down here to be parents to these homeless children. She said, "You have to give yourselves up and accept it as God's will, if that is to be your lot in life. God's way is always best." She said that together they came to the conclusion that it would not be God's will for them to "doctor" or see an infertility specialist. That gave me a lot to think about. Tonight as I was giving Pablos his bath and Marcinda had two of the toddlers in the tub, we had a discussion on childlessness. She said that if I'm worried that we'll never have children she would encourage us to adopt some, which is fairly easy to do in this country. She said there is an old Italian proverb, "The woman who havva no babies havva nothing." It doesn't seem fair to me that some couples have ten, twelve, or even sixteen children and others can't have any. But I guess it's true, as Barbara said, that God's way is best.

La Scenic Ranch

The sun came up this morning in a maze of mauve and pink glory and reflected on the cloud shrouded, mist-blue mountains in the distance. Well, we really are here on our "La Scenic Ranch," as it is called, and I still can hardly believe it's for real. It all happened so fast that it seems almost like a dream. Maybe sometime we'll wake up to find that it was.

My kitchen has plenty of windows, making it light and airy. There are built-in cabinets on two walls and the rest is painted in an off white, with dark brown woodwork. Our furniture is nothing to brag about, but we know it's only temporary. We are getting adjusted to milking these gentle brown Swiss cows. There are also several rows of pens waiting to be filled with calves. I enjoy helping in the barn, because being alone in the house is something to get used to again after all the noise and commotion at the orphanage.

I was real surprised to get a letter from Marcinda already—she says she misses us and wants to come and visit us sometime. She wrote that Pablos fell off of a chair and hit his forehead on a wooden toy block. He has a black and blue lump there now. I wish I could hold him again! Ninette drew a picture of a flower for me that was also included. It made me realize how much I miss them all.

Marcinda also sent this "recipe."

A RECIPE FOR LOVE

Melt a cup of closeness
With a pound of faith and trust
Add some tender moments
Stirring gently . . . then adjust
With a sprinkling of some laughter,
A few tears, some joy, a hug—
And hold forever after
In your heart to keep it snug.
                    —*Author unknown*

Wouldn't it be wonderful to have a baby of our own to love?

April 2
....
                              Yesterday   Nurse
Cassandra stopped in on her way to a mission station in Guatemala. I could hardly believe my eyes when I saw who was with her—lively little Hester from the orphanage! She gets to stay for four whole weeks. I am only now realizing how much I had been missing the childish prattle of the dear toddlers and

the noisy, happy chatter of the older ones. It just didn't seem right with no children around to cheer us up with the hurry and flurry of their activities and the pleasant distraction of their interests. Hester, or Esther, as Matthew calls her (he claims that to him Hester isn't a girl's name), is fair skinned compared to most of the other children of the orphanage, but has dark eyes and hair and an impish smile with a dimple in one cheek. She loves to help in the dairy barn, giving the cows their hay and feed and sweeping the alleyways. She is constantly on the move with her long black pigtails flying, a bundle of energy indeed. She likes to work and she likes to talk, which makes it interesting.

A wobbly little brown calf arrived in the barn yesterday (our first one) and Esther (I call her that, too) was so enraptured by it. Matthew and I were excited about it, too.

April 15

Matthew, Esther, and I went for a walk tonight in the timberland. We were amused to see Esther hopping and skipping along, flying from place to place almost like a butterfly. To her it was perfectly enchanting seeing the beauties of nature. She reminds me of Anne Shirley in the book *Anne of Green Gables.* I wouldn't be surprised but that she'll turn out to be every bit as good and lovable as Anne. Now all we need is a Mrs. Rachel Lynde (smiles). I can hardly believe that two weeks have passed already since Esther came—I'm afraid I won't be able to give her up when Nurse Cassandra comes for her. Matthew is quite fond of her, too.

.... I just made a round through my nursery, tiptoeing softly so as not to awaken my three sleeping babies. Can it really, possibly, be true? Nurse Cassandra's plans were changed somewhat when she came across these triplets that needed a home. Their mother is only sixteen years old and wants the babies back when she is older and married. She took them to the orphanage and Mama Barbara was kind enough to let me have them, sending Marcinda along to help take care of them. They are only four weeks old. They are three girls named Mae, Molly, and Mari. Their mother named them. We wouldn't have given the name of Molly—that is the mare's name. Mama Barbara let Esther stay, too, for she loves babies and can do a lot already for the care of them. Let's hope the babies sleep well tonight. They are so sweet and fragile and they need so much care. They're each bedded down in a laundry wash basket, for lack of cribs. Cassandra loaded her Jeep down with the supplies we would need—stacks and stacks of diapers, cases of formula, bottles and pacifiers, sheets and blankets. She said that if I get overwhelmed to send word, and she will take them back to the orphanage. That's a comforting thought. Well, we'll see. Marcinda and Esther are in bed already and Matthew will be in soon. Peace and quiet seems like a luxury already. And being carefree and helping in the dairy barn is a thing of the past, I suppose. But I'm happy.

.... It has been a hectic week. I won't be having much time for journal writing. Rocking babies is much more fun anyway! But you can't just toss them aside when you get tired of it! Seriously though, Marcinda, Esther, and I are having the time of our lives. Singing lullabies, mixing formula, patting for stuck burps, bathing, and changing diapers. Matthew helps quite a bit, too, and I believe he loves it as much as I do. I think I'll take the time to copy part of this well-known poem:

MOTHER'S LULLABY

Cleaning and scrubbing can wait till
    tomorrow
For babies grow up, we've learned to our
    sorrow,
So quiet down cobwebs and dust go to
    sleep—
I'm rocking my baby, and babies don't
    keep.
              —*Author unknown*

Marcinda found a "recipe" which she thought was cute—I'll copy it here, too, even though it won't apply to us right away—not until the children are older.

SUMMER RECIPE
FOR PRESERVED CHILDREN:

Take one large field, half a dozen children, two or three small dogs, a pinch of brook and some pebbles. Mix children and dogs well together. Put them on the field, stirring constantly. Pour the brook over the pebbles; sprinkle the field with flowers; spread over all a deep blue sky and bake in the sun. When brown, set away to cool in the bathtub.

—Author unknown

June 7

.... Nurse Cassandra stopped in today to see how we are making out and had some wonderful news for us—she is getting things cleared for us to adopt Esther! We are overjoyed; it's more than we dared to hope. We sure have gotten attached to her since she's been here. Cassandra told us that Cephas and Barbara had known before they sent Esther to us that she would be up for adoption before too long. They did us a big favor—so kindly and unselfishly as always.

Time to go—it's feeding time for the babies.

I reread that last sentence, and yes, it certainly has been feeding time for the babies. Several months of it.

Having church at our house comes around quite often because there are so few families here, but it's not as much work as if there were a larger group. On Sunday it will be our turn again, so I shouldn't take much time for this journal, even though I've neglected it for nearly half a year. The babies are all thriving—healthy as far as we know—except they all have a mild condition of clubfeet, which the doctor thinks will correct itself without braces. Mae is the biggest one, a pound heavier than the others. Mari has the most hair, and Molly smiles the most. They are identical, with round faces and blue eyes.

The menfolk of our community put up a small clapboard schoolhouse this summer, which is where Esther will go. Anna Lehman, a sister to Lynford, is the teacher. School starts tomorrow and Esther is very eager to start first grade, but Marcinda and I will sorely miss her. She is such a help with the babies. She had a bit of misfortune last week when out in the bean patch she stepped on a scorpion in her bare feet. The pain must have been severe, but she bore it bravely. We're so thankful that it wasn't the very poisonous kind that can be fatal. Matthew and I are only beginning to realize how hard it will be for us when it will be time for the babies to leave. We don't like to think about it, but it must be faced, I'm afraid. We always knew their mother would want them back eventually.

Matthew just found three slaughtered chickens lying in the barnyard this morning and came running into the house for his shotgun. There was a coyote in the chicken house! I made him wear gloves to dispose of (bury) the critter, for I'm worried about rabies. There have been a few cases reported lately in this area.

We also had a scare on Monday evening just before bedtime when a young man came to the door and demanded twenty-five *lempiras*. When Matthew refused (he knew there would be no end to it if we started giving out money, besides, we didn't have nearly that much in the house) the man became insistent, saying that his wife was in the hospital and he needed money for medicine. Seeing Matthew hesitate, he quickly added that his mother lived with them, too, and had broken her leg, and that his little girl was sick. We were beginning to doubt his story by then, and he kept on adding more calamities. He said that his son had been bitten by a snake and his uncle had hepatitis! We conferred together and decided to offer him a meal. But this seemed to anger the guy. It was money he wanted, and finally, in disgust, he left. We're so thankful he wasn't armed and violent.

My, we're having cool weather, the coolest we've had since we've been in Belize. Next we'll have to have mittens and scarves after all. Blankets are a necessity, too. Matthew has gone back to wearing his wool hat instead of his straw one. Today on the way to the store he met a group of gringos, and they all stopped and bowed very low. In this area, he found out, wool hats with a broad rim are a sign of prestige. Imagine!

Last week we had a surprise when a truck drove in containing a bunch of milk goats. There was one for each family in our group here, sent as a Christmas gift by Cephas and the others at Pleasant Valley. Now we'll have a taste of goat's milk. None of the others here have dairies so we're real glad for the gift, but Matthew and I decided we'd pass ours on to a needy family in the area. There are so many of them.

Golden Gem for Today:
Do not measure God's love
by thine own poor feelings,
nor think that His love slackens
when thine burns low.

January 15
.... Our excitement knows no bounds, for at this very moment Mamm, Daed, Peter, Sadie, and Crist are on their way to Belize and the La Scenic Ranch. The tears freely flowed when word came that they were coming— tears of happiness. Could it really be true? I hadn't

realized how much I was longing to see them again. Now that I know they are coming, time seems to crawl and my patience has completely flown away. It will seem like a miracle when we finally see them in my kitchen here! I know that I will spoil their welcome by crying when I see them.

February 1
.... The precious memory of my family's visit here remains like a pleasant glow of warmth and friendship. The week they were here passed as fast as the week before went slowly. Oh, how dear and familiar they all seemed! Mamm is a bit plumper and her hair a bit grayer. Daed has a few more lines in his brow. Peter is a good-looking, likable chap, and Sadie is a sweet, charming young lady. And Crist, lively little Crist, has already grown up, too. It's hard to believe. Sometimes I think it would be handy if we could stop the wheels of time, but it just keeps flying onward. They couldn't get over how adorable the babies are, what a good, dependable helper I have in Marcinda, and what a sweet little girl Esther is. She isn't mischievous anymore like she was at the orphanage. She likes school and is doing well. Priscilla and family sent a bunch of presents and wonderful news—they are planning to come and visit us next fall! I'm sure looking forward to that!

We discussed with Daed and Mamm the possibility of our buying this La Scenic Ranch. There is an option to buy on it now. We don't want to leave the country at the moment because Nurse Cassandra has sent word that the triplets' mother is now undecided. She might give up the babies for adoption after all and we might get the chance to adopt them! We don't want to get our hopes up too much, but can't help being excited. La Scenic Ranch is one of the better farms in this area, but the price is still very reasonable compared to back home. We very likely could get some financial aid from older church members. It seems like home now, and I'm satisfied to stay a few more years if we can adopt our family here. If more of our people settle in this area, the value of land will surely go up and it won't be hard to sell—that is, if we still want to. Our roots are starting to take hold here, something I wouldn't have believed possible two years ago. I suppose the longer we stay, the harder it will be to leave.

Here comes Mari, crawling over to me to be held—she's the most active one just now. Mae and Molly are sleeping already, so I'll cuddle her for awhile before I put her in—she took a longer nap than the others. Next month they'll have their first birthday. Can it be possible that nearly a year has gone by already since they entered our household? It was a hectic year, but I loved every minute of it. Maybe I can write more about my family's visit tomorrow—it was such a happy, interesting week that I wish I could recall every word and every single thing we did and every moment of it.

Another one of
those beautiful tropical sunsets tonight, changing
from breathtakingly awesome, to poignant as the colors gradually faded and the enchanting, velvety twilight fell. A silvery moon rose in the dusky darkness
of night. It's good to see Matthew taking the babies
for walks around the kitchen. They simply love it if
you take their hands, but if you let go they promptly
plop down. I don't think they'll walk alone much
before they are a year old. It's a good job for Esther,
but she gets her fill of it with the three of them. They
are at such a cute and lovable age. I don't let myself
think of having to give them up—it's just too unbear-
able. We'll just keep on praying that they don't go
back to unchristian parents and influences.

More about my family's visit:
   On the second day Sadie and I went for a long
walk, just to have one of those sisterly heart-to-heart
talks like we used to. It's been a long time since I'd
felt so carefree with Mamm there to help Marcinda
with the babies. It actually felt good to lay aside
motherhood's responsibilities and become a girl
again for a few short hours. I told Sadie of the dream
Matthew and I have of adopting a whole family of
children (at least a dozen) in this land before we
return. She thinks it's a good idea and said she
would like to come and help us for a year or two,
maybe after we have our dozen, and help us to move
back. I teased her a bit then, telling her she'd proba-

bly have half a dozen of her own by then, but she smilingly shook her head and said she has no prospects of a husband yet and is quite contented to have it stay that way. She always was such a sweet girl with the loveliest of personalities, and I know she'll bring happiness and cheer to others, whatever her walk in life may be.

The menfolk helped Matthew to put up more calf pens in the barn, so maybe in a few years we'll be able to increase our herd size if we buy the farm. They also got a lot of odd jobs done that had been waiting until we were not so busy. How can we ever return payment for all they did for us over the years and for their kindness and guidance? I suppose that they'll get their reward in heaven someday.

Mamm and I were finally able to visit to our hearts' content. Communicating by letters just isn't as satisfying, but it's better than nothing. There was many a time I would have liked to ask her something about the care of the babies, but couldn't, so I had to second guess. She assured me that I'm doing a good job, though.

The parting was hard, but now we have some more precious memories to store away for future use in our memory chest, when the longing to see them overwhelms us.

June 6
.... What a rain we had today—it just came pouring down in torrents and caused the creek banks to overflow. It reminded me

of being stranded on the mountains with Nurse Cassandra, and seeing the swift current in the creek made me shudder, thinking of our wild raft ride. There was no damage among our group, but in the valley they had some erosion of soil and flooding of fields. We had four inches in a short time!

The others of our group have been having trouble with chicken thieves lately. I suppose the heavy stone wall around our buildings is enough of a deterrent, although they could easily scale that if they wanted to. Perhaps they think we have some more barriers if we have a wall. I've heard that here in Central America the officials give people the legal right to shoot thieves. Imagine! Having been taught to be peace loving and non-resistant, it seems almost unbelievable. Would that be returning good for evil? I would sure think it could increase hatred and feuding among the citizens.

October 23
.... This must be the month for visitors! Three weeks ago Cephas and Barbara surprised us completely—I never dared hope they would be able to get away. But they have two Amish girls from Montana helping them now, so they took a well-earned vacation. On the day they arrived, we had just sat down at the dinner table when we heard a knock at the door. Esther was the first one to jump up and hurried to answer the door (she just loves surprises). She stood there dumb-

founded for a long moment, then with a cry of "Mama!" she sprang forward and threw her arms around Barbara, the tears running down over her cheeks. Barbara was teary-eyed, too, and it was only then that I realized what it must have been for them to be parted. They must both have had many a pang of *Heemweh* (homesickness), but Esther never complained. Both Barbara and Cephas were completely enamored with the three little girls toddling around our kitchen. They are already beginning to say a few words. But the best part of the visit was the message that Nurse Cassandra sent with them—the triplet's mother has given up her rights and signed them off for adoption. In a few months the proceedings will be legalized, and then no one can take them away! We both cried tears of happiness and gratefulness—we just couldn't help it. I'll copy a Bible verse of thankfulness here:

"It is a good thing to give thanks unto the Lord, and to sing praises unto Thy name, O most high" (Psalm 92:1).

October 24
.... I never did get our other visitors mentioned yesterday—I guess I realized I wouldn't have time after all and I wanted to save the best until last, for they were very important guests indeed—Priscilla and Henry. I think Priscilla and I were every bit as glad to see each other as Mama and Esther were! There was so much to say, so much

catching up to do. My only regret was that they couldn't bring the children along, for I've often longed so to see them all again. Priscilla is still caring for prison babies most of the time, but she felt that she needed a break, so they are doing some traveling.

She brought wonderful news—Rudy and Barbianne are the parents of another little boy named Joel. I understand better now how truly happy they must be and I rejoice with them. But I've found out that adopted children are just as loved as "flesh and blood" ones—there isn't a bit of difference.

Golden Gem for Today:
Trust God rather than thine own weak heart.

March 28
.... My, I sure don't get much journal writing done anymore, but since the triplets have their second birthday today, I thought I should. Marcinda and Esther had a lot of fun making a cake for them—putting on icing and decorating it, then putting on lighted candles. The babies were a bit young for a cake though, as Mae grabbed a lighted candle and burned her fingers slightly, and Molly grabbed a handful of icing to lick, and Mari, usually the most active one, just sat there and stared.

I have begun to help in the barn again sometimes, and tonight as we fed the calves, Matthew and I got to talking about Marcinda—how much she has done for us and what a big help she has been. We wondered what we could do for her to show her how much we appreciate it. She's almost like a sister to me—she even talks Dutch fairly well, a lot better than I know Spanish, I guess because she hears it more. She attended our church services several times, but prefers to attend the Spanish church down in the valley. She drives our horse, Pat, hitched to the cart, but attends only on our off Sunday in order to babysit for us when we go to church. We've told her over and over that it isn't necessary, that we'll manage somehow, but that's the way she wants to do it. She's under the impression that we're doing her a big favor by giving her a home, instead of vice versa. I suppose conditions in her aunt's home were very poor, according to some of the things Marcinda has told me. Their house was just a shack, with cornstalks piled on the roof to keep it from leaking. They lived on beans, rice, and tortillas, which I suppose nutrition-wise was not all that bad, but it lacked variety and taste. They didn't even have a garden, though there was room for one. *Ya well*, I must go and help to get the toddlers bathed and into their beds.

January 3
.... I apparently had nearly forgotten my journal, or else I was too busy. Is it really nearly three-fourths of a year since I last wrote? Ever since we bought this farm, Matthew has been busier than ever—maybe we should even get ourselves a *Gnecht* (hired boy) to help him.

We have decided to go back home to visit our families sometime this coming spring. I'm thrilled about it, but it won't be as easy to go as when we were carefree and childless. The children are going to stay at the orphanage until we get back, and Marcinda will be there, too, so I know they're in good hands. There will be a lot to do to get ready and I'm glad I have several months to prepare. We're planning to go by land instead of by sea this time—in a minibus with others of our group who are also going to visit their relatives.

June 11

....

This is Sunday afternoon, and all three babies are napping ever since we've come home from church an hour ago. Matthew reminds me that it is about time to stop calling them the babies, but it's hard to do. To me they are still babies anyway, even though they were three years old in March.

Now I'd like to write all about our trip—it was a wonderful, precious time for us, going back to our old homes and families. And yet, the best part was coming home and bringing our girls home from the orphanage and taking up our duties here again. I was glad that we could go in the lovely month of May and see the beauties of the springtime in Minnesota and Pennsylvania once again. We visited Matthew's parents first. What a bundle of memories it brought back, seeing his parents and younger brothers and sisters again! We visited

Birch Hollow School, where Rosabeth was in her last few days of teaching. We were able to attend the end of the year school picnic, and saw the lovely friendship quilt the parents had made for Rosabeth. We stopped in at Mahlon Swartzentrubers to see my former home, the *Daadi* (grandparent) end, which is empty at this time.

Then the long trip to Pennsylvania, to my old home by the creek. We were just in time for the blooming lilacs, and oh, the bittersweet memories they brought back. There were tears of both deep sadness and great joy. Matthew brought in armloads of them. We filled all the vases my family had, and they scented every room.

We all took long walks in the lovely, misty meadowlands where the grass was lush and green, and the buttercups as plentiful as ever. Robins sang sweetly from among the fragrant blossoming fruit trees, and it seemed to us almost like an earthly paradise. We even got to take in the first cutting of hay—the scent of new mown hay is incomparable. Before we left the earliest sugar peas and strawberries were ready, a real taste treat. The chirping martin birds, circling around their homes and swooping through the air to catch bugs, along with all the springtime beauties, brought on pangs of *Heemweh* (homesickness)—I realized that I had forgotten what I was missing while in Belize. We visited Priscilla and family, and my how they all had grown. If Priscilla hadn't sent photographs I would have been still more astounded. It was so good to get to know my sisters better, and Jethro, too. They all spent a lot of time at Daed's while we were there, and

Grandpa Dave's, too, so we could all be together more. Together we went to see Rudy and Barbianne and little Joel, whom we hadn't seen yet. I couldn't believe my eyes when I saw how James and Joanna had grown. James still remembered me, but to Joanna I was just a stranger. On the last evening we were there, Pam Styer came over, and all those we consider family sat in the big kitchen visiting and listening to Grandpa Dave telling his stories. Sadie and Crist hand cranked a freezer full of homemade strawberry ice cream— something we very seldom have in Belize. It seemed just like old times.

Once more we gathered a memory chest full of precious things to reminisce about, but like I wrote, the best part was coming back to our home. Be it ever so humble, there's no place like home.

Golden Gem for Today:
Many a weary pilgrim cheers his flagging steps
with thoughts of Heaven.

December 19
.... Wonderful news! Nurse Cassandra was here today and brought us a wonderful Christmas gift—or rather two of them. Two little boys, ages 5 and 6, brothers named Josef and Jolynn, and they're up for adoption! This is an answer to our prayers. Matthew especially has been longing for a son, and now we'll have two. And such a good daddy they will have! They are fair skinned, but with

dark eyes and hair. Their eyes are bright, intelligent, and alert, and they wanted to go off exploring almost as soon as they got here. They love to play in the barn, petting the calves, playing with the kittens, and gawking at the cows. We have a litter of nine-week-old Husky mix puppies, and when Jolynn came upon their nest in the straw, he gave a whoop of delight and scooped up an armful, as many as he could hold. Josef came running, too, and together they spent a long time happily playing with the puppies, while the mother looked on in half-amused tolerance. The boys can speak both Spanish and English (and we hope, before too long, Dutch) and are not a bit shy—they make themselves right at home. What a blessing that is!

Two more little souls to teach and to train in the nurture and admonition of the Lord—it sure is a big responsibility. I think I'll take the time to copy Susannah Wesley's rules for raising children:

HOW A GODLY MOTHER REARED HER NINETEEN CHILDREN:

What a saintly soul Susannah Wesley was! The mother of 19 children, including John and Charles Wesley, she dedicated her large brood to God and did not consult child guidance textbooks for guidance as to the preservation from evil in the lives of her children. Here are the sixteen rules she laid down, over 200 years ago, for keeping her many sons and daughters in the paths of righteousness.

1. Eating between meals is not allowed.
2. As children they are to be in bed by 8:00 p.m.
3. They are required to take medicine without complaining.
4. Subdue self-will in a child, and thus work together with God to save the child's soul.
5. Teach a child to pray as soon as he can speak.
6. Require all to be still during family worship.
7. Give them nothing that they cry for and only that which they ask for politely.
8. To prevent lying, punish no fault that is first confessed and repented of.
9. Never allow a sinful act to go unpunished.
10. Never punish a child twice for a single offense.
11. Commend and reward good behavior.
12. Any attempt to please, even if poorly performed, should be commended.
13. Preserve property rights, even in smallest matters.
14. Strictly observe all promises.
15. Require no daughter to work before she can read well.
16. Teach children to fear the rod.

I suppose number fifteen means to require no daughter to work outside the home until she has had some schooling. Her theories must have worked. All of her children turned out to be Christians.

At the moment, Marcinda and Esther are busy making small Christmas gifts for the younger ones. Even I may not see what they're doing, so I suspect they're making something for me, too. They share deep secrets and many a giggle.

We got a gallon of sorghum molasses and just now Marcinda is making taffy. Esther is at her side, wanting to stir the concoction and to learn how it's made.

I sit and marvel at our dear family, and thank God for them. I have no desire to move back home again at this time, but to stay until we have our dozen children. By that time our roots will probably have gone so deep that we won't want to move back.

There was an earthquake last week, but thankfully with only minor vibrations. Yet they lasted awhile and had us worried enough that we gathered outside in the yard. A calendar fell off the wall and the clock began to strike even though it wasn't time. There was no damage, and all's well that ends well, as the saying goes.

Our two little mischiefs (Josef and Jolynn) are thriving here, and have adjusted well. I call them mischievous, but they've done nothing worse than feed the horses too much grain between meals and penning a cat into the corncrib until it nearly died of thirst before Matthew discovered it.

September 19

Once more we have a new baby in the house, a sweet little blond, blue-eyed boy named Dylan. He is not entirely healthy as the others were. The doctor had a lengthy name for his condition that I can't remember, but it has something to do with his heart valve, and he will need surgery later on. But, oh dear, I'll have to finish this later, for I must go and tend to Dylan, he is beginning to cry, and it sounds like he can't wait another minute.

September 20

Word has spread through our group that a little four-year-old girl, the only daughter of a prominent physician, has wandered into the woods and is lost. According to reports they are rich people, and the child, whose name is Shana, had a governess to watch her. While Shana was playing with her kitten on the lawn, the governess fell asleep in a hammock. When she woke up, Shana and her kitten had disappeared. A search party was formed this morning—there is a call for more volunteers to comb the woods. Matthew and a few other men in our community offered to go. A native neighbor from a mile away will be driving to the spot and will take them along. I'm anxious to hear whether she is found when they return tonight.

Dylan is doing well, but takes more care than the average baby. (He will be six weeks old tomorrow.)

Mae, Molly, and Mari love to hold him, but Esther tops them off in that. She'd spend every waking moment with him if she could, and is a real good help in caring for him. We are all very happy to have him.

September 21
.... Matthew returned home last night, weary and footsore, with the discouraging news that the child has not been found. Every effort was made to cover each square foot of the mountain, and every thicket and underbrush searched out. They tramped all day, and this evening bloodhounds and a helicopter were brought in. I feel sorry for those parents. That little girl must be the same age as the triplets. I've often been thankful for that stone wall around our property, but the little ones have to be watched in the barn, too. That poor governess. How awful she must feel, knowing it was her responsibility to watch the little girl.

Golden Gem for Today:
Prayer is putting ourselves consciously into God's presence.

September 25
.... Matthew spent two more days helping with the searching, and on the evening of the third day Shana's body was found, curled up in a spot of dense thicket. Yes, life was

gone, and the tears flowed freely when the news was heard. Matthew attended the funeral today down in the Spanish church. The mother the child is English, and she handed out sheets of paper to everyone who wanted one, with the following poem neatly typewritten:

"O what do you think the angels say?"
Said the children up in heaven.
"There's a dear little girl coming home today
From the earth where we used to live in.
Let's go and open the gates of pearl,
Open them wide for the dear little girl,"
Said the children up in heaven.

"God wanted her here where his little ones
    meet,"
Said the children up in heaven.
"She shall play with us in the golden street.
She has grown too fair, she has grown too
    sweet
For the earth we used to live in.
She needed the sunshine, this dear little girl,
That gilds this side of the gates of pearl,"
Said the children up in heaven.

"So the king called down on the angel's
    dome,"
Said the children up in heaven.
"My dear little darling, arise and come,

To the place prepared in the Father's home,
The home my children live in.
Let's go and watch at the gates of pearl,
Ready to welcome the new little girl,"
Said the children up in heaven.

"Far down on earth, do you hear them weep?"
Said the children up in heaven,
"For the dear little girl has gone to sleep,
The shadows fall and the night clouds sweep
O'er the earth we used to live in.
But we will go and open the gates of pearl
Oh, why do they weep for the dear little
        girl?"
Said the children up in heaven.

"Fly with her gently, O angels dear,"
Said the children up in heaven.
"See, she is coming. Look there, look there,
At the jasper light on her sunny hair,
Where the veiling clouds are riven.
Oh hush, hush, hush, all the swift wings furl
For the King himself at the gates of pearl
Is taking her hand, dear tired little girl
And is leading her into heaven."

—*Author unknown*

October 24
.... Yesterday we had

some important visitors—Marcinda's brother Juan, and little brother Freddy, carrying Polly the parrot in a cage. We were greeted by her cries of "Buenos dias, Buenos dias!" and "Pleased to meet you!" plus a lot of new phrases they have taught her. I had to think of a saying I once read, "So live that you would not mind giving the family parrot to the village gossip."

It meant a lot to Marcinda that they came, and we all appreciated their visit. Their dad has remarried to a kind-hearted woman, and Freddy has gone to live with them. Juan just came back from the seacoast and is temporarily staying with the family. Freddy and Esther still know each other, too, and seemed glad to see each other again. They stayed for dinner and we had a good visit until mid-afternoon when they left.

November 5
....
Dylan is scheduled for his surgery next week since he has gained enough that they feel safe to go ahead with it. He turns blue easily, but the doctor says that will change after his successful surgery. I don't understand all that they will do, but it has something to do with a valve. He smiles easily and coos in such a sweet, friendly way. The triplets are a big help with him these days, for school has started again and Esther isn't here as much. They love to rock and sing to him. I can hardly believe how much they have changed these past months. At age two and three they were still into

everything, what one didn't think up to do, another one did. They had to learn to get along with each other and to share their toys.

Matthew is enjoying it having two helpers in the barn—Josef and Jolynn spend as much time with him as possible. Next year Josef starts school already. My, our family is growing up fast. Matthew and I are truly thankful from the bottom of our hearts for our little family, and hope that God will send us more to love and to train up in the nurture and admonition of the Lord.

Mamm sent me a little poem that is a gentle reminder to be patient and gentle with the little ones:

Lord, teach us patience while the little hands
Engage us with their ceaseless small demands.
O, give us gentle words and smiling eyes
And keep our lips from hasty, sharp replies.
Let not weariness, confusion and noise
Obscure our vision of life's fleeting joys
Then, when in years to come our house is still
No bitter memories its rooms shall fill.

—Author unknown

She wrote: "There is no greater task than that of being a parent; to have innocent little souls entrusted to our care, to lead them heavenward day by day. It's an awesome responsibility, to teach them and train them, tell them Bible stories, to influence them for the good while they are yet in the tender, pliable years. I have to think of the words of Jonathan Edwards, a minister of the 1700s. He wrote: 'Never lose one moment of time, but improve it in the most profitable way you possibly can.' That goes for child raising, too, I'm sure, for they grow up so fast, soon they will be gone and our chance over."

November 10
.... Time seemed to go very slowly as we sat in the waiting room at the hospital yesterday while they did Dylan's surgery. I wished I had brought some hand sewing to do, or anything to keep busy and to help pass the time. Matthew and I talked (to keep our minds off the tension) of our years here in Belize, and about whether we'd ever want to move back, then about each one of our children, their different personalities and characters.

Then when we finally were taken in to see Dylan, he was in an incubator, still sleeping, with tubes attached here and there, and he was on oxygen. Such a sweet, fragile little bundle. We longed to hold him, but weren't permitted to yet. Matthew went home with the same taxi we had come with to do the chores, but I stayed for the night to help care for Dylan as much as permitted. He is stabilized now, and doing as well as can be expected. The surgery was successful, and we thank God for it. Today Marcinda came in to the hospital so I could come home. She'll stay until tomorrow when Matthew and I go back in. We're hoping to be able to take him home soon.

I'm spending most of my time here in the hospital with Dylan and Matthew spends some time here, too, so Marcinda has the responsibility of the family at home much of the time. She says that Josef and Jolynn are more mischievous when we are gone. Yesterday they sneaked off down to the creek, and were crossing it on a fallen log over the creek when Jolynn slipped and plunged headlong into the water. Josef made a grab for him and was dragged into the water, too. Luckily it wasn't too deep for them to wade to shore. Then in the afternoon they got into a shouting boxing match, and Josef swung his fist at Jolynn, who jumped aside fast enough, and Josef's fist hit the wall with an awful crunch, as Marcinda worded it. (No, raising a family is not all roses, there are plenty of tough times, too.)

Matthew reported that he took them along to the store, with Pat hitched to the cart, and they got to shoving and tussling, and Jolynn fell off and the wheel went over him. He climbed back on, laughing, none the worse for his tumble.

The worst thing that happened, though, was yesterday when Josef drank some Basic H liquid, thinking it was mint tea. He was gagging and coughing and big bubbles came out of his mouth. Marcinda pounded him on his back, and was very much afraid that he would suffocate. He couldn't talk, could hardly even breathe, and she was nearly frantic. He took a drink of water, and then there was more gagging and bubbles. Finally he vomited for real, and then it was over. He suffered no more ill effects from it. I told Marcinda that this is why mothers and dads—and mother's helpers—get gray.

November 13

Dylan smiled for us today, which was very encouraging. He's not supposed to cry hard and we're doing all we can to prevent it. We met and had a talk with Dr. Francisco, the father of the little girl, Shana, who perished in the woods. He thanked Matthew for helping and attending the funeral. He was a very friendly, personable man. He even took us to another floor to meet his wife, who works as a nurse at the hospital. They'd like to come out to our farm sometime to meet the rest of our family. I think he is interested in adopting a child, too, but his wife is not ready yet. Maybe it seems to her too much like replacing Shana.

Golden Gem for Today:
*Faith's eye rests and is riveted
on the Cross of Calvary.*

November 16

We brought Dylan home today, a delicate little bundle to care for day and night, but we do it gladly. We hope that now he can grow well and strong, into a husky lad with color in his cheeks and a sparkle in his eyes. Nurse Cassandra stopped in this afternoon, she intends to be in the area for a week and will check on him several times. She's well pleased with how he's doing and said that the adoption can be finalized soon. She has been such a blessing to us these past few years, and we can never even begin to repay her for her kindness. The same with Marcinda—it warms our hearts to know that she chooses to stay with us even though she could easily find a better paying job. She says she loves the children like her own, a blessing indeed to us all.

January 1

Dawn is just now breaking on another New Year's morning, and this verse comes to mind: "This is the day the Lord hath made, we will rejoice and be glad in it."

I received a letter from Sadie yesterday, and this verse was included:

NEW YEAR'S WISH

All that is beautiful, all that is best,
Joy of activity, calmness of rest,
Health for life's pilgrimage,
Strength for its strife.
Sunshine to brighten
The pathway of life.
Love that is tender, friends who are true,
This is my New Year's wish for you.

She wrote that Mamm had a gall bladder operation, but is at home and doing well now. Also the surprising news that Peter is writing to a girl from Minnesota, namely Laura Swartzentruber, who was my scholar, a cousin of Perry's. I think she's a very nice girl indeed. Maybe we'll get a chance to attend two weddings there soon, Peter and Laura's and Milo and Anna Ruth's, and to visit both our families once more. But sending our children to the orphanage won't be as easy as it was last time. Maybe we could get someone to come here to help Marcinda and Esther with the care of the family and to do the chores.

August 15
.... I suppose it was bound to happen sooner or later—that thieves cause us trouble again. When Matthew went to the barn this morning, his prize registered brown Swiss bull was missing. There were truck tires up to the barn (the gate was open) and that told us the story. We've had so little thievery in our area lately that we no longer bothered to lock the gate, and now we wish we had. But perhaps they would've gotten in anyway. The funny part of the story is that by noontime the bull was back in his pen! What happened? Tonight we heard that a truck going down the Hillside Road had its brakes give out and it ran into a steep bank. The truck overturned and we presume that the bull rolled out. He is unhurt, but scratched

up a bit. Apparently he had enough sense to head for home right away, and the gates hadn't been closed yet, so he went right back where he belonged. Matthew and Josef and Jolynn hitched Pat to the cart tonight, and drove down to look at the truck. Its windshield was knocked out, and he believes it was quite beat up to start with. Let's hope it discourages those thieves from more thievery.

Dylan has now had his first birthday and is walking. He doesn't seem like the same child since his surgery. He was a thin, blue baby and now he's rosy-cheeked and chubby and beginning to say a few words. He is the sunshine of our home, or rather, I should say, one of them.

May 19
.... Journal writing isn't one of my hobbies these days, for my entries are few and far between. I guess I'm too busy caring for my family. Mae, Molly, and Mari are really into playing dolls these days. They have a little table with four chairs (they allow Dylan to sit on the one), and they have a forty-piece china tea set that we got them for Christmas. They spend many an hour entertaining themselves thus, and seem to never get tired of it. Mamm and Sadie sent them each a homemade Raggedy Ann doll, with homemade dresses, aprons, and caps, and these are their favorite ones. It's fun to listen to their chattering when they play pretend house or church.

Josef and Jolynn are real Daddy's boys by now, and can help a lot with the chores already. Guess we won't need to get a *Gnecht* (hired boy) after all. They don't spend much time in the house if Matthew's out working. Esther has turned out to be even more interesting than Anne of Green Gables. There's never a dull moment when she's around, and she's already as good a helper as Marcinda with the younger ones. We have been richly blessed with our wonderful family, for which we are profoundly thankful. The crushing disappointment of not being able to have children of our own has turned into a blessing.

November 18

....

Today is Peter's wedding day, and next week is Anna Ruth and Milo's, and we aren't able to be there for either of them! My thoughts travel to Minnesota, though, and I keep thinking, as the hands of the clock go round, of what they are probably doing just now. At 8:00 this morning I thought, "Now everyone is being seated, and Peter and Laura, hand-in-hand, walk into their place of honor." A little later, "Now Dad Isaac has begun the sermon, and how I wish I could hear it." "Now the ceremony—they are standing up to be married, and pronounced man and wife." Then, "They're all seated at the long table, with the delicious feast spread before them." All day I kept thinking of them, and following them in thought. It sure takes a lot of giving up to miss both of the weddings.

Now, for the reason we couldn't go. Nurse Cassandra has brought us another baby, a little girl named Rosita. This one is a colicky baby, and we're thankful there are four of us to walk the floor with her and rock her. I have to wonder if this was the reason her mother gave her up for adoption! She's a sweet little thing, though, even though she hasn't a bit of hair yet, not even any eyebrows. She's three weeks old and we're hoping she'll outgrow her bellyache soon. Thankfully, Dylan doesn't take much care—he sleeps all night and plays contentedly most of the day.

February 20
.... Mamm sent me a poem, and I think it's sweet, so I'll copy it into my journal:

WHERE DID YOU COME FROM?

Where did you come from baby dear?
Out of the everywhere into the here.
Where did you get your eyes so blue?
Out of the sky as I came through.

What makes the light in them sparkle and
   spin?
Some of the starry spikes left in.
Where did you get your little tear?
I found it waiting when I got here.

What makes your forehead so smooth and
   high?
A soft hand stroked it as I went by.
What makes your cheek like a warm white
   rose?
Something better than anyone knows.

Whence that three-cornered smile of bliss?
Three angels gave me at once a kiss.
Where did you get that pearly ear?
God spoke and it came out to hear.

Where did you get those arms and hands?
Love made itself into hooks and bands.
Feet, whence did you come, you darling
   things?
From the same box as the cherubs' wings.

How did they all just come to be you?
God thought about me, and so I grew.
But how did you come to us, you dear?
God thought of you and so I am here.

—George MacDonald (1824-1905)

We thank God for bringing her to us. We can
more fully appreciate her now that she's over her
colic at last and sleeps well. She has even grown a bit
of hair already.
    Just now she's sitting in her infant seat, content-

edly cooing, and already seems so bright-eyed and alert, noticing what's going on around her. The children are all different, yet all so precious.

November 5

It's twilight, a peaceful time of the day. A long gray bank of clouds hang over the shadow shrouded mountains, and the evening birds are twittering good nights to each other as they settle on their perches for the night. Today was Molly, Mae, and Mari's first day of school, and they happily followed Esther out the lane, carrying their lunch boxes and waving good-bye. Esther reported tonight that they did very well and weren't a bit shy, maybe because their older sister was there and they had each other for company. They can already say their ABC's, write their names, and count to fifty, thanks to Marcinda. I think they'll be reading soon. Won't that sound cute to hear them read aloud?

November 12

Can it really be two years since I last wrote in my journal? Time just keeps marching on, making us older every year. We are now back from our trip to attend brother Crist's wedding, and I want to write all about it. He got married to Preacher Emanuel's daughter Elizabeth, and the wedding was at her house, close to Daed's.

To make it worthwhile traveling that great distance, we arrived in Pennsylvania in October already. They were having beautiful, sunny, golden, Indian summer weather, and the very first day Sadie and I went for a walk along the creek where the golden leaves were floating lazily down into the water and the squirrels were chattering and scolding as they gathered acorns and shell barks for the winter. We walked all the way to the swinging bridge. Wild geese were winging their way overhead and blue jays were calling from the trees. Everything brought back memories from my girlhood. There were sweet memories and sad ones, some bittersweet—of remorse and learning the hard way, but with restitution and peace at the end.

Sadie is thinking of opening a small bulk food store—I think it's a great idea.

I'm sure that everyone would want to shop there, for she's such a lovable, cheerful person.

In the orchard there were piles and baskets of freshly picked apples, some to be made into cider. I ate my fill of them—the Maiden Blush were my favorite. Piles of pumpkins on the side of the barn hill made a colorful display. The marigolds and mums hadn't frozen yet, and made a lovely splash of yellow and orange color. We visited all our old friends and family in the neighborhood—it's unbelievable how all the children have grown. Grandpa Dave is aging fast, but we have all the memories with him to cherish. Time to go, maybe I can finish this tomorrow.

Back to our trip. The wedding day was cold and blustery, with a cutting north wind. But we enjoyed every minute of it. Now I have two sisters-in-law on my side to get to know better. At least we can write to each other, even though we can't visit often. Mamm told me a wonderful bit of news: they plan to come and visit us in the spring to get to know our family better! Now that's really something to look forward to! They haven't even seen the younger ones yet. Mamm had a Doves 'n Hearts quilt in the frame, and Priscilla, Miriam Joy, Barbianne, Annie, Sadie and I (even Pam Styer sometimes) spent more than one afternoon together visiting and quilting. More precious memories to store in our memory chest to bring out and treasure later on. I'm beginning to realize more and more what all I miss out on by being so far away. Ya well. Rosita just came in crying, with two skinned knees from falling on the driveway, and I must go tend to her.

November 14

Maybe I can finish writing about our trip now while Marcinda and Esther entertain the younger ones by telling stories. We traveled on out to Minnesota next, to Matthew's old home place, and we had a wonderful visit with his parents, brothers, and sisters. They too would like to come and see our home and family sometime, but would like to see us move to Minnesota. We also visited Owen Hershbergers and Enos Millers, and went to Milo and Anna Ruth and Peter and Laura. We went to see the old Millstream Orchard Farm we lived on for the first year of our married life, and it did stir up a longing to move back. Enos Miller is still renting ten acres of it, but the farm will come up for sale again next year, and he says if we want it, it's ours. We explored the place, and it was all just as we remembered it—the three lilac bushes, the low wall out front by the road covered with honeysuckle vines, the three little ponds in the meadow and orchard, the climbing roses on the trellis at the porch that would make a dazzling crimson display in June, the house with the cupola on top, and the blue spruce trees out back. I know I could make myself at home there, should we decide to move. It would be hard to sell this La Scenic Ranch though. Yes, it will be a hard decision and Matthew says it might take us a year to make up our minds. I guess it all depends on whether Nurse Cassandra will bring us more children, for we can't move out of the country until a certain length of time after the adoption is legalized. She is not well at the present time, and the talk is that she might have leukemia, but we're hoping it's not true.

Rosabeth is still the Birch Hollow schoolmarm and enjoying her job. She had been dating for awhile, but that fell through, and she, like Sadie, says she is happy and contented. She is a blessing to all who are fortunate enough to know her.

.... We're having cool
weather with a drizzling rain coming down part of the
day. Glad we're back from our camping trip!

Since we are thinking of leaving our La Scenic
Ranch here in the shadow of the mist-blue mountains
and moving back to Minnesota, we'll try to take in as
much as we can of this land of enchantment before we
go. Matthew and I had long dreamed of going on a
camping trip, exploring the mountains, and sleeping
outside on the mountainside, enjoying the tropical
beauty and scents, and the warm, balmy night breezes.
But at first, the thought of the possibility of meeting up
with poisonous snakes deterred us (well, me anyway).
Then we had gotten our fill of that kind of thing when
we were stranded up in the mountains and had to
escape in a wooden raft with Nurse Cassandra and
Freddy. But, on Monday Matthew brought up the old
dream again, saying that there's no time like the present. He said that the poisonous snakes are mostly in the
coastal regions, and with a bit of precaution there
shouldn't be any danger of meeting up with one. And
so we began to make plans for our camping and hiking
trip.

Hettie (as we sometimes affectionately call Esther)
and Mae, Mary, and Molly opted to stay home with
Marcinda, and so just Josef and Jolynn went with us.
We started out early on Tuesday morning, just as the
sun was coming up over the horizon. The beauty of the
sunrise was breathtaking, but we eyed it a bit warily,

for we were hoping for nice weather. And sure enough, before we had even gone the four miles to the foot of the mountain, a sudden, unexpected shower came up. It wasn't just a sprinkling. It was a heavy tropical downpour of warm rain that soaked us to the skin in a few minutes. But then, almost before we knew it, the sun was shining again. Josef and Jolynn were in high spirits, cavorting around playfully and enjoying the rain. Afterwards, when the sun came out, they wrung out their dripping wet shirts and pranced around in the sun's warmth. Matthew said they had better preserve their energy, for they would be needing it before the day was over. In a surprisingly short time our clothes were dry again and we walked in comfort. Roosters were crowing from the dwellings we passed, and we met a man with a burro loaded with wares he was taking to market. A flock of parakeets swooped down into a tree above us, and then flew away with a whirring of wings. The air was fresh and clear after the rain, just right for hiking. At the base of the mountain we followed the well-worn trail that crosses over the mountain, pushing aside the dense vegetation that grew out over the trail. There were a lot of green leafy ferns and giant trees with trunks of immense size. The rainfall in the mountains is heavier than in the lowlands, and so the vegetation is denser and the wildlife is abundant. Birds sang in the tropical paradise, just as joyfully as they do on a fine May morning in Daed's bush land along the creek back home. By the time we reached the higher elevations we were huffing and puffing, and the water from our canteens was mighty refreshing. We sat on a large rock and rested for about twenty minutes, wishing that the dense vegetation would not obstruct our view down over the surrounding valley and countryside. What a magnificent view we would have had!

Josef and Jolynn were still feeling energetic, raring to go on and conquer the mountainside, but I was beginning to think that maybe I should have stayed home. I wondered how much farther it was to the top. But the rest refreshed me, and soon we were on our way again. After another hour of climbing, sometimes pulling ourselves along by roots and tree branches, we heard the sound of falling water. Around the next bend a cascade of water came into view through the leaves on the trees. Coming closer, we saw that it was a waterfall at least thirty feet high, with white water tumbling down over the rocky mountainside and whirling into a pool, then disappearing into a rocky crevice in the ground. Matthew said he thinks it erupts out of the ground again farther down the mountain somewhere. There, by the side of the cascading water, we perched on a rock and ate our lunch while enjoying the beauty of our surroundings. We refilled our canteens, and after a short nap under the sun-dappled foliage, we set out again, for the boys were eager to reach the summit. Soon the trail merged with a zigzagging switchback road, and we saw a thatched-roof house on up the trail in a clearing. Matthew decided that we should stop and visit with the owners of the house, and so we timidly knocked on the door. For awhile, nothing happened, and then we heard a shuffling sound inside. The door creaked open, and an old stoop-shouldered man with sparse white hair to his shoulders peered out at us, blinking in surprise. "Who is it?" he asked, seeming a bit bewildered. Matthew explained to him who we were and what we were doing so far up in the mountains, and then a kindly smile lit up the old man's face, and he opened the door wide and welcomed us inside. He had twinkling blue eyes and seemed very glad to see us—he said it was a long time since he last had visitors. His home was very primitive and his furnishings sparse, but he pulled out chairs and benches for us and did his best to entertain us royally.

Ya well, I guess I'll have to finish about our camping trip later, for Rosita just awoke from her nap, and it's nearly time to start supper. We're having tortillas, beans, and rice, which is standard fare for this country, but we're also having something rare and elegant—a golden sponge cake which Hettie made for Thanksgiving Day, and it's frosted and decorated, too. It turned out high and light, much to her delight.

I'll take the time to copy an inspirational verse yet.

Golden Gem for Today:
*If you climb upward on the rays of the morning sun or land on the most distant shore of the sea
where the sun sets, even there God's hand will guide you and His right hand will hold onto you.*

November 25

We had a lovely Thanksgiving Day with so much to be thankful for. But lately my thoughts have been traveling homeward to our parents and the big family gatherings, the bounteous feasts of fellowship with friends and relatives. Will we be back among them again sometime in the future? Time will tell. Hettie is longing to be able to go, for to her it would be a great adventure. She is one that is apt to be a bit restless. She dreams of traveling and doing great things for others. Matthew told her that she should "Sew first piety at home," and that "Godliness with contentment is great gain." She is a good daughter and tries to be obedient, and I hope that her dreams will be fulfilled someday.

And now I'll continue the story of our hike over the mountains. The old man, whose name was Rolf Fernheid, was very accommodating. He served us a drink of fresh, warm goat's milk and buttermilk biscuits, and was friendly and talkative. We sat on benches made of four-foot planks nailed to round chunks of wood. The table in the middle of the room was also made of several planks nailed onto a three-foot high tree stump. He also served us goat cheese and honey to go on the biscuits.

We spent the night in Rolf's house, and the next morning traveled on to the summit of the mountain. There was a magnificent view from up there; it was well worth the climb. On the next mountain ridge we could see a little village clinging to the hillside surrounded by steep little fields, where a farmer was plowing with a pair of oxen. We decided to press on and pay them a visit. We found the people to be very accommodating and friendly there. They all invited us to stay for dinner, and the hard part was to decide whom to honor by accepting the invitation to eat at their house. We finally chose the family that lived in the most prosperous looking house—a neat adobe, a Spanish house with a lawn in front. The woman of the house was from Texas, and she is now an instructor in an agricultural school. She was really friendly as was her husband, who is a native Belizian with a handlebar moustache. They have two daughters, ages 10 and 12. They were both shy and sweet with large dark eyes. We were served a delicious meal—a vegetable stew and hamburgers on white rolls—something we hadn't tasted in years. It was all very interesting and we were almost reluctant to leave that bit of luxurious hospitality. They even invited us to stay for the night, but we declined, saying we had to get back to the family at home. And so we started off, waving to all the villagers who had come to see us off, and began our hike up over the mountain. That night we sure got our fill of camping. When it began to rain lightly and became quite chilly, I wished we had accepted the invitation to stay at the village. We built a fire with all the dry wood we could find, which warmed and cheered us as we cooked cornmeal mush for our supper. But during the night the fire died down and we woke up feeling chilled to the bone and quite miserable. The approach of dawn the next morning was a welcome sight, as the rosy glow in the east beckoned a new day. The drizzle had stopped by then, and we quickly packed up to head for home. The closer to home we got, the more our pace quickened, and when at last we could see the rooftops of our La Scenic Ranch, we all cheered, for it was a most welcome sight. The girls and Dylan were very glad to see us, and we were thankful that everything had gone well while we were away. Marcinda and Hettie had whitewashed the chicken coop and cleaned the whole house with the triplets' help. Dylan and Rosita gave us a rousing welcome, and it was so good to be home. Home Sweet Home.

Well, the youngsters have been begging to go for an outing for some time, and Matthew has promised Josef and Jolynn to take them fishing down at the creek, and so we decided to do it tonight. I'll copy a verse yet, and then help the girls pack the picnic supper and help to carry it down and get the bonfire started.

Golden Gem for Today:
We are thirsty, Lord,
and we long for the refreshment
only You can give. May we not settle for the
temporary satisfaction the world offers,
but reach for the living water only You can give.
Whosoever drinketh of the water
that I shall give him shall never thirst;
but the water that I shall give him
shall be in him a well springing up
into everlasting life.

November 26

....

Tonight the sun set

in a maze of red and pink glory over the usually mist-blue mountains that surround us, reflecting its changing colors on the highest peak. Matthew and the boys helped to clear a small field of brush for a neighbor, chopping down all the vegetation with a machete. They had a bad scare when Jolynn nearly stepped on a coral snake that slithered out of the grass. The neighbor quickly killed the snake with his machete, and they kept a sharp look out for its mate. Coral snakes are swiftly poisonous! But they hardly ever come out in the daytime. Perhaps it was disturbed by the grass and brush being chopped down. I'm glad that didn't happen before we went on our mountain hike—we probably couldn't have enjoyed it as much, or perhaps wouldn't have had the courage to go at all.

December 23

Once again I think of the Christmas season back home. The reason for the season is the same here as there—the birth of our Savior, his coming to earth as a babe in a stable, and the angels singing from the heavens, "Peace on earth, good will towards men." But I think, with a pang of longing and nostalgia, of the wintry scene with the snow-covered landscape, the swirls and mounds of beautiful, fluffy white snow covering everything. I think of the sleigh rides on the bobsled with the bells jingling merrily, watching the youngsters skating on the pond, swirling and gliding over the smooth ice, and of attending a comfort knotting or quilting and listening to the latest community news. Breathing in frosty cold air, and breathing out puffs of frosty whiteness. Hearing the screeching sound of carriage wheels on soft snow. Coming in from the cold and crowding close to the big black range, trying to absorb its warmth—or better yet, warming your toes in the bake oven. My thoughts often travel to those things and I have to wonder—do I have *Heemweh* (homesickness)? Matthew too, often talks of old-time memories, and we find ourselves discussing the pros and cons of moving back. We want to do what is best for the children and to follow God's leading.

I'll take the time to copy a few verses for my Golden Gem for today:

Golden Gem for Today
Be careful for nothing, but in everything
by prayer and supplication with thanksgiving
let your requests be made known unto God. Also:
And the peace of God
which passeth all understanding
shall keep your hearts and minds
through Jesus Christ our Lord.

Millstream Orchard Farm

Another two years have passed since my last journal entry, and now there are only a few more pages to fill. I am sitting here by the open window in the kitchen on our old Millstream Orchard Farm in Minnesota, close to our good neighbors, Enos and Betty Miller. A fragrant, lilac-scented breeze is blowing in the window. Robins and song sparrows are joyously singing from the treetops, and the sunrise is splendid, tingeing the sky with pink and orchid hues. Matthew and the boys are nearly finished with the milking and will soon be in for breakfast, which Esther is preparing. Marcinda is no longer with us—before we left Belize we all attended her wedding. She married Victor Delgado and they live in a cottage near La Scenic Ranch. Our family of eight children are all healthy and growing, which is much to be thankful for. Sister Sadie has been living with us since we are here, and with her help we are managing to keep them clothed and fed, and are trying to raise them in the nurture and admonishment of the Lord. I found a lovely poem that I'd like to copy here, for it's a reminder of

how swiftly the years pass by and how fleeting are
the years of their childhood.

YOUR CHILDREN

Take time to laugh and sing and play
And cuddle them a bit.
Tell them a story now and then
And steal a little time to sit
And listen to their childish talk
Or take them for a little walk.

You do not know it now—but soon
They will be gone—the years are swift—
For life just marches on and on,
And heaven holds no sweeter gift
Than a small boy with tousled hair,
Who leaves his toys just anywhere.

Take time to hear their prayers at night
To really cherish and enjoy
A little girl with flaxen curls,
And the small wonder of a boy.
They ask so little when they're small
Just love and tenderness—that's all.

—*Author unknown*

Honeysuckle time! I'm sitting here on the old stone wall enjoying the sweet fragrance and counting my blessings. Matthew has taken the boys down to the pond to fish and Sadie is playing a game in the yard with the girls and Dylan.

The children have all adjusted nicely to our move, and we all like living on this scenic farm.

We've found out that our old neighbors, Ken and Jocelyn Bates, have moved into the city, and that their cute little cottage has been for sale for quite awhile with no buyer—until last week, that is. Guess who? Sister Sadie and Matthew's sister Rosabeth! They plan to buy it together for a home of their own. They've become good friends since Sadie came to live with us, and when they saw the cottage, they were as enchanted as I was the first time I saw it. They'll share the house and Rosabeth will continue with her job of teaching school, while Sadie will continue to help us out several days a week, and on the other days work at a bulk food store. It seems too good to be true to have them living so close, permanently, for I'm sure that both of them will be a blessing to our family.

I think I'll fill the last page of my journal by copying a part of "A Fine Morning Prayer" out of *The Prayer Book for Earnest Christians*:

O Lord, since you,
are our God and Creator,
direct our life and walk
according to Your holy and divine will.
All our works and deeds are in Your hands.
We commit ourselves into Your hands.
O holy Father!
with body and soul and all that we have.
Rule over us, and advance the work of our hands.
We ask this, O holy Father!
in the name of your dear Son, Jesus Christ,
who promised us that you would respond favor-
ably when we call upon you in his name,
praying with reverent and believing hearts.

Credits

The Golden Gems are adapted from Charlotte Mary Young, translator and editor, *Gold Dust* (Chicago, 1880: reprint, Philadelphia: Henry Altemus, n.d.), a collection of devotional thoughts for the holy and happy life. *Gold Dust* is translated from the French series *Paillettes d'or* (1868ff.), by Adrien Sylvian (1826-1914).

Prayers from Leonard Gross, translator and editor, *Prayer Book for Earnest Christians* (Scottdale, Pa.: Herald Press, 1997), are used by permission.

The Author

The author, using the pen name of Carrie Bender, is a member of an old order group. She lives with her husband and children among the Amish in Lancaster County, Pennsylvania.

Bender is also the author of the popular Miriam's Journal Series, featuring the day by day adventures of a middle-aged Amish woman, and the Whispering Brook Series, books about fun-loving Nancy Petersheim as she grows up surrounded by her close-knit Amish family, friends, and church community.

Readers can reach the author by writing Herald Press, 616 Walnut Ave., Scottdale, PA 15683.